Wild Ghost Chase

THE GHOST DETECTIVE MYSTERIES - BOOK 7

JANE HINCHEY

BP
BAYWOLF PRESS

Baywolf Press
PO Box 43
Ingle Farm, SA, 5098
Australia

AUTHOR'S NOTE

Hey! Welcome to the weird and wacky world of my imagination. I hope you enjoy your time here.

If you love anything supernatural as much as I do, then you're going to enjoy the journey ahead - at least I think you will.

Wild Ghost Chase is the seventh book in my Ghost Detective series, with more to come, so make sure you sign up for my newsletter to get notifications on when the next book is ready.

You can sign up for my newsletter here:
Janehinchey.com/subscribe

Okay, ready to weave some magic and solve some mysteries?

I'll see you on the other side!

xoxo

Jane

Want to get an email alert when the next Ghost
Detective Mystery is available?
Sign up for my newsletter today,
https://janehinchey.com/ghostthehallsgiveaway
and as a bonus, receive a FREE e-book of
Ghost the Halls!

ABOUT THIS BOOK

As a private investigator and ghost whisperer, I ask myself many questions—why can I see dead people? Can I wear purple to my own wedding? How do you get peanut butter out of a raccoon's fur? But '*who killed Gianna Tate*' was never among them. Until now.

1

"*I* really didn't think this through," I said, turning to the dead woman riding shotgun in my Honda CR-V. She glanced at me, eyes running over my fancy dress costume.

"The straw is a nice touch." She gave a nod to the bright orange straw I'd crammed under my battered hat. It had seemed like a good idea at the time to come as a scarecrow to Firefly Bay's annual Scarecrow Ball. But oh my lordy, the straw! Thankfully, I'd only shoved it under my hat, not all over, because straw? It itches like you have a bad case of something contagious. That requires medical treatment. And ointment. Lots and lots of ointment.

The woman's costume, on the other hand? She was a fairy-tale princess, complete with a massive ballgown that took up almost the entire front of my car and puffed around her like a tulle-filled meringue. The gemstones on the bodice sparkled in a ray of light that cut through the windshield, twinkling in the fading light as the sun dipped over the horizon. I didn't sparkle. I itched.

"Cinderella?" I asked, nodding at the white gloves that reached beyond her elbows and the crown perched upon her short blonde hair. Technically, Cinderella had long hair, but who was I to quibble?

She lifted a bare shoulder in a half shrug. "Not really."

"No?" My brows shot up, creating friction between the straw and my hat and scraping my skin. "Who then?" Shoving an index finger beneath the band of my hat, I scratched.

"I'm the fairy godmother," she deadpanned.

I didn't think my eyebrows could physically reach any higher on my forehead, so color me surprised when they hit my hairline. At least, that's what it felt like. It could've been the tight hat and abundant amount of straw cutting off circulation, yet oddly, not the itching sensation. I patted my brows with my fingers, reassuring myself that they were still in situ while eyeballing the woman incredulously.

Gianna Tate was a ruthless divorce attorney with a passion for making money. At least, that's what I'd heard. I'd never had personal dealings with her before other than to say hello, but sitting in front of me, all I saw was a beautiful woman, mid to late fifties, blonde hair cut in a stylish pixie, subtle makeup that accentuated her blue eyes, impossibly thick and dark lashes that made me think they were false, and a slim figure that told me, for a dead woman, she liked to keep in shape. She did not, in any way, resemble the fairy godmother I remembered from my childhood.

I turned back to the windshield, stuffed a couple of Cheez-Its into my mouth, and pondered the turn of events that found Gianna in my car. Dead, obviously. Unless the blood marring the front of her pale blue gown was fake. Costume blood. But she'd appeared out of thin air, so I felt reasonably confident in my initial assessment.

"So…" I swallowed my mouthful of Cheez-Its. "You're just a straight-up fairy godmother? Not the horror version or anything?"

"Horror version? What on earth are you talking about?" She fluffed the tulle around her, seemingly genuinely oblivious to the blood and her non-living status.

"Actually, I'm glad I caught you," she said, as if she hadn't just materialized in the front seat of my car wearing a ball gown with bloodstains.

"Oh? Why's that?" Without a doubt, I was one hundred percent expecting Gianna to say she'd been murdered and wanted me to find her killer. That's how it usually worked. Ghosts found me, and I'd find out who killed them. Assuming they'd been murdered, of course.

Ever since my best friend Ben had died and come back to haunt me, I'd been able to see ghosts. I am a ghost magnet. Or, more accurately, a ghost detective. I help the dearly departed solve the mystery of their death, giving them peace of mind and justice, which allows them to cross over.

Except for Ben, who'd chosen to stay. And when I say haunt, I don't mean it in the clanging chains and moaning in the dead of night way. Ben just hangs out with me. It's almost like normal. Except he's dead. And only I can see, hear, and speak to him. Did I mention I can also talk to—and understand—Ben's cat, Thor? I agree—the whole thing is pretty freaky. We don't really know why, other than Ben's old neighbor dabbled in witchcraft, and the night Ben was murdered, she did a little something-something that resulted in... this. Me, talking to and seeing ghosts.

"I want to hire you," Gianna said.

I shoved another Cheez-It in my mouth. "Yeah? What for?" *Here it comes.*

"Someone is attempting to blackmail me, and I want you to find out who and shut it down. But this has to stay on the down-low. No one can find out about it. At all. Ever."

I stopped chewing. My hand—already in the

Cheez-It box for another serving—froze. "Blackmail?" I hadn't been expecting *that*. "Tell me more."

"I received an email demanding money, or they'd release risqué photos from my youth."

I began chewing again. "*Are* there risqué photos from your youth?"

She crinkled her nose. "Who knows? My youth was a very long time ago. Needless to say, I have no intentions of paying, but I can't have this interfering with my work. I don't want our law firm dragged into anything untoward, so I figured I'd hire a private investigator. Your name came to mind."

"Why not go to the police?"

She shot me a look. "Because if there *are* risqué photos, I want them destroyed. The police would take them into evidence."

Of course. But now, she was dead. At the hands of the blackmailer? Why would the blackmailer kill their meal ticket? You can't get money from a dead person.

"Who sent the email?" I asked.

She rolled her eyes. "If I knew that, I wouldn't have to hire you." She waved a hand around, narrowly missing the box of Cheez-Its. "It came from one of those anonymous email accounts. The bogus ones anyone can create."

"Right. What did it say? Exactly. Instructions for a money drop? A deadline?"

"It was a couple of sentences. It's probably best if you read it for yourself."

"Probably," I agreed, my mind spinning with possibilities. Gianna was a successful divorce attorney and partner at Beasley, Tate, and Associates. The same firm my sister-in-law, Amanda, worked at as a paralegal. But behind every successful case, there was a loser on the opposing team. Mostly disgruntled spouses who'd battled it out in a courtroom and lost, thanks to Gianna. She probably had a list a mile long of people who'd wished her dead.

"Shouldn't we be going?" She tapped her wrist where her watch would be if she weren't wearing the gloves.

"Just waiting on Galloway," I said. "Cheez-It?"

Her chin tilted in the air. "You know those are bad for you, right?"

I dusted Cheez-It dust off my hands and figured while we waited for my fiancé, one of Firefly Bay's best detectives and, may I mention, smokin' hot to boot, we may as well get to the bottom of Gianna's recent demise.

"Tell me about your afternoon."

She frowned. "Why?"

"So I can get a sense of who you are, your usual routine, that type of thing," I lied. If I could jolt her memory, get her to recall her murder, we just might solve this mystery quickly, and I'd still get to go to the ball. Selfish, but what the heck, if I was going to create a makeshift wig out of straw, it was only fair I got to go to the ball.

"Today hasn't exactly been a usual day," she said.

"Because of the ball?" I asked, reaching for another Cheez-It from the box I had crammed between my seat and the center console.

"Obviously. I had a few things to take care of in the office this morning—"

"Do you usually work Saturdays?" I cut in.

She lifted one shoulder. "Usually, yes. The office is quiet, and it gives me a chance to go over case files, et cetera, for court on Monday."

"Right. So, you went into the office. Then what?"

She was silent for a moment, then tapped her wrist again. "We need to get going. The firm holds a private soiree before the ball, and this year, it's at my house. I need to be there."

"You have a party before a party?" I wasn't sure if it was genius or merely extravagant.

She inclined her head. "Correct. It's a way for us to thank our staff and to have a bit of fun together before the ball. The ball is more networking and schmoozing." Her voice had an edge of flint, indicating her irritation that we weren't moving, and I could see what others saw, the steely lawyer who brooked no BS.

"You don't like the networking and schmoozing?" I

prodded, wondering if I was poking the bear, for her mood seemed to have soured.

"When you are as good at your job as I am, you become public property. That can get... tiresome." Then a sly grin curled the corner of her lips. "But profitable."

"So, nothing... *unusual*... happened today?" *Like you getting killed, for instance?*

"What on Earth are you trying to say?" she demanded, head snapping and eyes pinning me to my seat with a red-hot glare. I gulped. Her eyes could strip you bare and flay your soul. I would not want to be on the opposing side of Gianna Tate in a courtroom.

Ignoring her glare, I plowed on. "You want me on the case, then I have to ask the questions. Sorry."

"Fine." She gave a brief nod and settled back in her seat, staring out the windshield. The view wasn't spectacular. We were in my driveway, waiting on Galloway to get changed into his costume, only he was taking his sweet time about it. Which was kinda a moot point since Gianna had shown up; there'd be no ball. We needed to find her body.

I had a feeling that when news broke about Gianna's demise, Amanda was going to be a royal pain in my ass. Not that she wasn't already. Amanda was on a crusade to *fix* me. Not that I needed fixing. I'm clumsy, not broken, and we'd clashed over that little fact on more than one occasion. Currently, we were enjoying a cease-fire, but Gianna being murdered was going to upset the delicate balance we'd established. I sighed and shoved more Cheez-Its in my mouth.

"So, after the office, you went home and got changed?"

She looked down at the ballgown, smoothing her hands over the voluminous skirt. "I guess? I don't really remember. How did I get here?"

"No idea. You look lovely, by the way."

Gianna softened like butter on a hotcake. "Thank you." She pulled at the short strands of hair at her nape. "I was going to wear a wig but in the end decided against it. They're so hot. And itchy."

I snorted. "You should try straw. Gives itchy a whole new meaning."

The front door of my house opened and closed, and a nervous thrill rushed up my spine. Leaning forward against the steering wheel, I watched as Galloway strode purposefully toward me. He was the sexiest darn scarecrow I'd ever seen. I loved him for agreeing to be in what had to be a certain degree of discomfort, judging by the straw he had poking from his sleeves and trouser legs, just so that we'd match.

He must've felt me ogling him, for he glanced up, caught my eye, and grinned, and it was all I could do not to fan my face and swoon.

"Oh, my!" Gianna had no such qualms.

Remembering our uninvited spirit currently riding

shotgun, I jerked my thumb, indicating Galloway should take the back seat. His step faltered ever so slightly before he gave a slight nod and altered his trajectory to accommodate.

"You look fantastic." I twisted in my seat to give him an approving once over once he'd settled into the back seat.

"Thanks. So do you. Love the makeup." He winked, and I remembered that I'd colored in the tip of my nose, round red dots on my cheeks, drawn on eyelashes like a cartoon doll, and one of those slasher mouths with the stitches. I'd felt pretty cute until Gianna had turned up all Cinderella-like in my front seat.

Galloway had his phone in his hand and a sheepish look on his face. "Babe, I hate to do this, but...."

"We can't go to the ball," I finished for him. I tilted my head toward the passenger seat, indicating my dead passenger. "We have Gianna Tate with us."

Galloway shot a look toward what appeared to him to be an empty seat, then his phone, and back to me.

"Was the call about Gianna?" I asked, biting my lip. It was tricky when the ghost you were helping didn't know they were a ghost. Galloway, bless his cotton socks, was a quick study. "We've been called to an incident at Gianna's house," he confirmed.

"Oh, good!" Gianna twisted in her seat to beam at him. "You can drop me at my place, and I can catch the limo to the ball with everyone else. This is working out perfectly."

And that's how I arrived at Gianna's mansion. Unlike Cinderella and her pumpkin with her mice, but instead in a metallic blue Honda CR-V, with a hunky scarecrow and a ghost.

2

"*A*udrey!"

Sliding out from behind the steering wheel, I self-consciously straightened the bib of my dungarees, aware that my scarecrow costume was a far cry from glamorous. Not that Amanda cared. In fact, I'd never seen my sister-in-law quite like this before. Distraught, but also a vampire.

"Hey, Amanda." I gave her a quick hug before taking in her costume. Long black dress, her blonde hair replaced by a black wig, her face caked in pale makeup with hollowed eyes, exaggerated veins painted around them, and blood-red lips. Not to mention the fangs.

"I just can't believe it." Her voice shook as she clasped onto my hands, her grip uncomfortably tight. "It's such a shock."

"I know," I said, glancing at my brother, Dustin, rubbing a hand up and down his wife's back. "Count Dracula, I presume?"

He nodded, face somber beneath his heavy makeup. "Yeah. Amanda is Lady Dracula."

We stood in front of Gianna's mansion—because to call it a house was a disservice. The place was b-i-g huge! It had one of those circular driveways where you drove in one way and out the other without ever having to reverse. In the center, a water fountain. I secretly coveted a driveway like this. Only seeing it bathed in red and blue flashing lights wasn't precisely how I pictured it.

Galloway stepped away to speak with one of the officers who stood waiting. Gianna spied the stretch limo parked with doors open, the chauffeur twisting his hat in his hands, and sped off to settle herself inside, excited to be going to the ball.

I turned my attention to Amanda, "Can you tell me what happened?"

She sniffed and released my hands, running her fingers beneath her eyes and smudging her makeup. I'd never seen her disheveled before. I really wanted to pull out my phone and take a photo, but I couldn't bring myself to do it. If only I wasn't such a pushover.

"I don't know, other than she's dead."

"Who found her?"

Amanda glanced around, her bloodshot eyes

landing on a woman dressed in a La Calavera Catrina Day of the Dead costume. "Carolyn did. We were all in the ballroom when the limo arrived. Gianna had gone upstairs for something, not sure what, to touch up her makeup or fix something with her dress? She didn't say. She just said she had to quickly do something and went up to her bedroom."

"But didn't come down." It wasn't a question, but Amanda answered anyway.

"No." She cleared her throat. "So, yeah, the limo arrived, and we came out here to get in while Carolyn went upstairs to get Gianna."

Galloway caught my attention, beckoning me over. Giving Amanda one last reassuring pat on the shoulder, I excused myself and joined him on the front porch.

"Is she here?" He kept his voice low, for my ears only.

"She's in the limo, and she doesn't know she's dead," I whispered.

"Damn. I was hoping she could identify her killer, and we could wrap this up quickly."

"So, we can go to the Scarecrow Ball?" I asked hopefully.

"So we can appease the press," he deadpanned.

"Oh! Right. Okay." Of course. It was a high-profile case, I chastised myself. Gianna Tate was not only wealthy but a very successful attorney and business owner. The press was going to be all over this. Even as I thought it, a van with a local television logo on the side pulled up behind my car in the driveway.

"Jacobs, deal with that. Set up a perimeter to the street," Galloway barked.

Officer Sarah Jacobs gave a curt nod and approached the van, gesturing them to move, shaking her head and holding out her arm, pointing toward the street. I heard her say *crime scene* and *no comment*.

"Let's get inside." Galloway took my elbow and guided me over the threshold. Gianna's mansion was... well, it was just like you'd imagine a mansion to be. The foyer rivaled any five-star hotel, complete with a dominating chandelier dangling overhead and huge vases filled with opulent floral bouquets.

"Nice place." A grand staircase swept up either side of the foyer, meeting at the top to form a runway. "But big for one person. She must've rattled around in here all on her own."

"Her body is upstairs. This way."

I followed Galloway across the foyer, pausing to look through a set of French doors into what had to be the ballroom Amanda mentioned. It was a massive room with a sparkly disco ball hanging from the ceiling, still spinning, sending shards of light bouncing off the walls. There were sofas, chairs, and side tables placed strategically around the room, along with a bar with a mirrored backboard and liquor shelves.

Streamers draped across the ceiling, and helium-filled balloons bounced on the ends of golden ribbons.

Realizing I wasn't behind him, Galloway swiveled on his heel to come see what I was looking at. "Looks like she did a lot of entertaining," he commented. "This is quite the setup."

"She told me it was her turn to host the pre-party this year. Before the Scarecrow Ball, they throw a soiree for the employees of Beasley, Tate, and Associates."

"That'd explain the wait staff out front with the guests." Placing a hand on the small of my back, he guided me up the staircase, turning right at the top, down a hallway to a set of massive double doors at the end. One door stood open, and we eased through.

"Don't touch anything," Galloway said to me, accepting a pair of latex gloves from Sergeant Jamie Powell, who met us at the door.

"The coroner is still en route," Powell said, giving me a quick nod in greeting. "The body is in the dressing room."

"Start interviewing everyone who was here, staff and guests. Put them all in the ballroom, but turn off the disco ball and music first. No one is to leave, understood?"

"Yes, sir!" Powell departed, and I followed Galloway, who pulled on the gloves as he walked, the latex snapping against his skin sounding unnaturally loud in the silence of Gianna's bedroom. I eyed the walls, wondering if she had soundproofing installed.

"She hired me, you know," I said.

Galloway stopped, and I ran into his back, bouncing off and almost landing on my rear if he hadn't shot out a hand and caught my wrist as I flailed around. "What?"

"Well, she was *going* to. That's what she said. Only she died before making it official. But I'm taking the case anyway."

He snorted. "Fine. I guess I can let you help."

"Help?" My voice shot up an octave. "Did you say help? I can solve the blackmail case *and* this garden variety homicide."

Galloway laughed. "Don't worry, Fitz, we'll probably close the case before you."

"Really! Well, perhaps you'd like to make things... interesting?" I narrowed my eyes, seeing if he'd take the bait.

"Whoa. Wait. Are you saying you want to wager on who solves the case first? That's sick. What do I win?"

I grinned. "Dinner at the restaurant of the winner's choosing."

"And free back rubs for a week."

"Deal."

"Deal."

Galloway leaned in, lowering his voice. "Not a word to the coroner about any of this. She'll shoot us."

"Secrets, murder, and gambling. Three of my favorite things."

"I didn't know you gambled."

"I don't, but I needed something to fit."

"Yeah, yeah. Good one. Okay, let's do this." He took a step forward, stopped, and swiveled to face me. "First, a couple of ground rules."

I rolled my eyes. "Okay, fine. What?"

"I'll let you follow me around the crime scene, providing you share anything Gianna tells you."

Hmmm. My ghost whispering capabilities were my secret weapon—but not overly helpful if the victim didn't remember anything. On the other hand, having access to the crime scene wasn't to be sniffed at.

"Okay, fine, whatever."

Galloway studied me intently. "Just so we're clear, we're *sharing* intel."

Crossing my fingers behind my back, I smiled my sweetest smile. "Yes, dear."

He held my gaze for a few seconds before smirking and continuing to the crime scene with me hot on his heels.

Gianna Tate's dressing room was the size of my bedroom. It was a dream. The outside walls of the room housed rack upon rack of dresses and suits. An island bench with a marble top that ran down both sides sat in the middle of the room. Alongside the bench was Gianna's body, face down on the carpet, one arm outstretched toward the door. She was in her fairy godmother costume.

Galloway crouched by her side while I stood by her feet, watching him examine the scene. "She was heading for the door," he said. "Leaving the dressing room when she was surprised by her attacker." He glanced at me and the no doubt blank look on my face. "The direction of her body, the way her arm is outstretched in front of her, tells me directionality."

"Ooooh. So, she wasn't trying to run away, is what you're saying. She trusted her killer. It was someone she knew. Someone who was meant to be here."

"You catch on quick."

I winked. At least, I hoped I did. There were times when I couldn't quite pull off a wink and delivered a screwed-up blink instead. "I had a good teacher."

"If you two have quite finished," a woman's voice said from behind me, making me jump.

Galloway stood. "Coroner."

"Detective. What do we have?"

"Gianna Tate, fifty-five, female, found dead by a colleague approximately thirty minutes ago."

"And this is?" The coroner shot me a look that I couldn't read. Either she was annoyed at having an unidentified person at her crime scene, or she was trying to work out my costume. Possibly both.

"Private Investigator Audrey Fitzgerald," Galloway said smoothly, unruffled by the coroner's frosty demeanor. "Audrey, this is our relief coroner, Rachel Sanderson."

"What is a PI doing at my crime scene?" You'd think she'd stepped in dog poop the way she said it. And now I knew why Galloway didn't want her getting wind of our little wager. She probably *would* shoot us.

"Gianna was my client." I figured the coroner wouldn't bother herself with digging deep enough to ascertain if that were the truth or a lie. I was in that gray area—partial truth.

"What would an attorney of Gianna Tate's caliber want a PI for?"

"Blackmail."

She arched a brow, and I cursed her ability. "Explain."

"Someone was attempting to blackmail her. She hired me to find out who."

Coroner Rachel Sanderson was grating on my nerves. Still, it appeared she was satisfied with my answers, for she didn't demand that I leave the crime scene, which I was exceedingly grateful for. If I was going to beat Galloway at cracking the case, I needed a good look around to see for myself what went down.

"Don't touch anything," Rachel said, setting down her case and snapping on her gloves. She felt along Gianna's spine and around her neck and skull. "No blunt force trauma, as far as I can tell. Let's roll her."

I bit my tongue to keep from blurting out how

Gianna died. The sheer volume of Gianna's dress was no doubt hiding the pool of blood beneath her body, but as soon as they turned her over, the cause of death would be self-evident.

"Ah," Rachel nodded, seeing what I'd seen the moment Gianna had appeared in my car. The bloodstain on the front of her dress and the small hole in the fabric of her bodice.

"What are you thinking? A knife?" Galloway asked, leaning forward to get a good look at the wound.

"Hole's too small for a knife. A small, round object like an ice pick or screwdriver."

"Or a bullet."

Rachel swung her head to look at me. "You think she was shot?"

I shrugged. "It's a possibility, isn't it?"

"No exit wound." Rachel sniffed, turning her attention back to the body. "No stippling around the wound. Highly doubtful she was shot."

I looked at Galloway, who was watching me. I held his gaze. "Seems to me that she was taken by surprise. That she knew her attacker. She wasn't attempting to get away. Rather, she was heading *toward* the door, where we presume our killer entered the room."

"Your point?" If Rachel's voice got any frostier, I'd be sporting icicles.

"That if someone approached you holding a weapon, you would turn away and attempt to run."

"A screwdriver or icepick are weapons of opportunity. She may not have perceived the killer as a threat."

"Granted," I conceded. "But to stab her, you'd have to hold it like one, right? And Gianna is a top-notch lawyer with, one would assume, pretty good observational skills...."

"So, she'd notice if someone she trusted was approaching holding, let's go with an icepick, in a manner she deemed threatening, then she'd be turning away. She'd attempt to put the island bench between herself and the other person," Galloway finished.

"Exactly." I crossed my arms. "Hence why I think she might have been shot."

"We'll find out for sure when I do the autopsy," Rachel snapped. "You'd better not be dropping straw on my crime scene."

My hands shot to my head, where the orange straw was still poking out from beneath my hat. I'd briefly forgotten the discomfort, but the itch was back tenfold now that Rachel had brought my attention to it.

3

*A*manda was speaking. I know this because her lips were moving, and her hands were gesturing, only with my scalp itching and her vampiric makeup distracting me, I barely took in a word. With nothing more to see upstairs, I'd headed down to the ballroom, figuring I'd listen in on the witness statements the officers were gathering, save myself some legwork, and potentially beat Galloway in solving the case. I was particularly looking forward to a week's worth of back rubs.

"Are you even listening to me, Audrey?" Amanda wailed, punching me in the shoulder.

"Ow!" I complained, rubbing where the skull ring she wore had connected with my flesh.

Amanda was immediately full of apologies. "Oh,

my gosh, I'm so sorry. I forgot I was wearing this stupid thing."

"Relax. It's fine." I eyeballed my sister-in-law, all twitchy and with bloodshot eyes. It was fascinating watching her unravel but also sad. Despite our differences, I didn't like seeing her so distressed.

"Take me through everyone who is here tonight," I suggested. "And who they are dressed as, cos honestly? Some of these costumes are amazing, and the makeup is exceptional."

Amanda clasped her hands together, lowered her head, and took a deep breath before raising her chin and looking me dead in the eye.

"Beasley, Tate, and Associates were founded eighteen years ago by Felix Beasley—he's over there, dressed like a mobster. And Gianna Tate. Back then, it was just Felix, Gianna, and Carolyn."

"Carolyn?" I pounced on the name. "Isn't she the one who found Gianna's body?"

"Yes." Amanda pointed. "That's her over there, dressed as La Calavera Catrina. She's our receptionist."

I wished I could get my eyebrows to quit moving because each time they shot up in surprise, my forehead itched like the devil, and I couldn't help but scratch. My surprise was that if Carolyn had been with the company for eighteen years, why was she still in the receptionist's role?

"How old is she?" It was difficult to distinguish

Carolyn's features with the white, black, and red sugar skull makeup or guess her age. Still, I figured she was older than most people here tonight from her sensible flat shoes and the stoop of her shoulders.

Amanda looked up at the ceiling while she flicked through her database of a brain before pulling out the answer and returning her gaze to me. "She's fifty-eight."

"Pretty senior for a receptionist."

"Don't be ageist." Amanda immediately defended her co-worker.

"It's merely an observation," I protested, eyeballing the older woman in her black dress with red roses in her hair and painted face. She was slim and looking at her now, I could see a certain crepiness around her neck. While I wouldn't say she looked frail, she certainly didn't match the zest and vitality of the young woman by her side. "Who's that next to her?"

"That's Chloe Hawkins. She's our family law assistant and office manager."

Chloe had also chosen a day of the dead theme. Only her costume was the zombie version. The gray face makeup with the skeleton shading was exceptionally well done.

"And how old is Chloe?"

"She's twenty-two."

Again with the eyebrows. Shoving a finger beneath the brim of my hat, I scratched. "Let me make sure I've got this straight. So, we have Carolyn, the receptionist who has been with the company for eighteen years. Then we have Chloe, the office manager who has been with the company...." I trailed off, inviting Amanda to fill in the blank.

She obliged. "Around six months."

"Wow. And Carolyn wasn't mad that you employed someone not only young enough to be her daughter but that she was overlooked for the position?"

"I wasn't involved in hiring Chloe, but there has never been any animosity, so I'm guessing it's never been an issue." She flicked the dark hair of her wig over her shoulder, her eyes darting around the room.

I made a mental note to ask Gianna about it.

"Okay, so who is Marilyn Monroe over there?"

"That's Jessica Watson. She's Gianna's paralegal. The company is divided into trust and estate planning, led by Felix, and business and family law, run by Gianna."

"Gotcha. So Gianna's team consisted of Jessica, her paralegal, and you said Chloe was the family law assistant and office manager, yes? Is that it for Gianna's team?"

"No, there are also those two zombies. Jack Ayers, attorney, and his wife Caitlin, his legal assistant."

"So that leaves you—you're Felix's paralegal, yes? And then that gigantic fluffy squirrel? Who's that?"

Amanda giggled. "That's Hailey Thomas, attorney,

and her legal assistant is Evie Riley, dressed as Mia from the Princess Diaries."

"And that guy?" I pointed toward the one man in the room not in costume.

"That's Chris Haiden, attorney. He's our floater."

"Floater? What does that mean?"

"He's not assigned to any one division. He goes where he's needed depending on caseload and leave."

"And he doesn't have his own assistant?" Meaning no one to arrange a costume for him.

"No, he utilizes existing staff. Only the partners have paralegals. Hailey and Jack have legal assistants, but not paralegals."

I nodded, casting my eye over the imaginative costumes the employees of Beasley, Tate, and Associates were wearing. They'd embraced it and had gone all out. Except for Chris Haiden. Besides not having any administrative support, was there a reason he didn't wear a costume?

"Who do you think killed Gianna?" I asked Amanda.

Her eyes bugged out on stalks, and she clasped her hands to her chest. "What? No one here! It wasn't one of us." She shook her head vehemently. "It can't have been."

"Oh? Why not?"

"Because we were all here, in this very room. The

only person to leave was Gianna and then Carolyn, who went to get her when the limo arrived."

"You're all each other's alibi is what you're saying." Darn. Someone in this room had to have killed Gianna, but if no one left, how, exactly, did they manage it?

"That's precisely what I'm saying."

Uh-oh. Amanda had her paralegal voice on. She clearly didn't like the insinuation that one of her colleagues was behind Gianna's murder.

"I suggest you interview the wait staff," Amanda sniffed, back ramrod straight. "They were hired to cater the party."

Gianna chose that exact moment to turn up. "Why are you all still inside?" she demanded, standing with hands-on-hips and eyeballing her team. "The limo is waiting."

"Who hired the wait staff?" I asked Amanda, ignoring Gianna. I really hoped she wouldn't make a scene. When ghosts made scenes, they were impossible to ignore, and then *I* was the one who looked like a loony tune.

"I think it was Carolyn. If not her, then probably Chloe."

Officer Sarah Jacobs approached, notepad in hand. She gave me a brief smile and a head nod before turning her attention to Amanda. "Do you mind if I ask you a few questions?"

"Not at all. I've just been filling Audrey in on who is who."

"Maybe we can go over here?" Officer Jacobs guided Amanda toward a chaise lounge in the corner of the ballroom.

"What's that all about?" Gianna asked.

Quickly checking no one was in earshot, I put my hand to my face, pretending to scratch my nose as I answered. "There's been an incident. The police need to ask a few questions."

"What sort of incident?"

"You don't know?"

I got that cold glare again. "I wouldn't be asking if I did, now would I?" She tsked.

"Tell me about Carolyn." I nodded toward the older woman who was being guided to a chair by the giant squirrel.

"What about her?"

"Amanda was telling me she's been your receptionist for eighteen years. I would have thought you'd have promoted her to the office manager role rather than hiring externally."

Gianna smiled and nodded. "Ahh. Yes. Carolyn spends her days at the office making everyone's life a little easier," she said with genuine warmth. "Her years of experience and enthusiasm to take care of those around her make her the perfect fit as the point of contact for incoming clients."

"She sounds like a gem. And she didn't mind? Not being promoted?"

"Carolyn is at the end of her career. She's been in the workforce since nineteen eighty-four, initially in Rochester in New York, where she worked and raised a family. She worked hard. Too hard, I think. Eventually, she missed the ocean and came home to Firefly Bay. The timing worked in our favor when she joined us as our receptionist. But Carolyn never had any ambition to climb the corporate ladder. She'd done that in Rochester, and now she just wanted a nice stable job that she could leave at the door and go home to her cats every night." Gianna began pacing in front of me. "Why are you asking? Do you think she's behind the blackmail attempt?"

"Do you?"

Gianna snorted. "Absolutely not. Carolyn is family. Heck, they're all family. I'm sure you're aware I've never married or had children. Beasley, Tate, and Associates is my baby."

"So, you're one hundred percent sure no one here meant you any harm?"

"Ninety-nine percent."

I frowned. "Ninety-nine percent?"

"There is one staff member who I know is not entirely happy," she admitted. My eyes landed on the only staff member not in costume.

"Let me guess, Chris Haiden?"

She nodded. "Yes, Chris."

"Why's that?"

"He's brought it up a couple of times now, both with Felix and with me, that he doesn't want to be a floater. He wants in on family law exclusively."

"Does that mean a pay rise?"

She shook her head. "No, it means he won't be assigned to trust or estate clients anymore."

"He doesn't like doing that type of work?"

"He says he's always wanted to pursue family law and has a particular interest in child support cases and parental rights and responsibilities. We try to give him those clients when they come in, so...?" She tilted her head to the side, mouth twisting as she chewed the inside of her cheek.

"Is there a reason you can't assign him?"

"Because then we wouldn't have a floater, and we need one for when we're busy and to cover vacation and leave."

"Ahh. So he's stuck in that role until a vacancy becomes available in the family law division?"

"Correct. He knew this when we hired him."

Gianna raised her arm and waved at Chloe, hurrying across the room to speak to her. Of course, Chloe couldn't see nor hear Gianna, but Gianna didn't notice and continued an animated one-sided conversation with her employee.

I slowly made my way around the room, pausing to

listen in on the various conversations, most of which consisted of everyone's shock and horror at what had occurred. But one thing was for sure. Make that two things. Firstly, Gianna remained one hundred percent oblivious to the fact that she was no longer living, and despite everyone talking about it, she was in glorious denial. The second thing? Everyone, including the wait staff, had been in this very room when Gianna was murdered, meaning none of them could have done it.

"Hey." A hand on my shoulder had me practically jumping out of my skin.

Hand to my chest to settle my frantically beating heart, I turned to Galloway. "You startled me!"

"Apologies. Can I borrow you for a minute?"

"You sure can." I leaned into his side. He wrapped an arm around my waist and led me out of the ballroom and into the foyer.

"Well?" He cocked his head toward the ballroom door. "What do you think?"

Right. We'd agreed to share intel. How was I going to win if I told him everything? But then again, right now, there wasn't much to tell.

I chewed a nail, my mind running a mile a minute. "I don't see how anyone present in that room could be the killer. They're all alibiing each other. They say no one left the room. Except for Carolyn, who went to tell Gianna the limo had arrived and found the body."

"Hmmm." Galloway ran his fingers over his

stubbled jaw. "She could have killed her. Claimed to have found the body but, in fact, killed her."

I glanced through the open doorway toward Carolyn, who was sitting in her Day of the Dead costume staring at her hands. She'd drawn a skeleton outline on the back of her hands and fingers that was now smudged from all the hand wringing.

"I guess she could have." I had to agree it was possible, although I didn't think it was probable. "Although her motive is pretty flimsy."

"She has motive?"

"Not really. Apparently, she's been in the receptionist role for eighteen years, since Beasley, Tate, and Associates first opened. Six months ago, they hired Chloe as a legal assistant and office manager."

"And you think that upset Carolyn?"

I scratched my forehead. "I told you it was flimsy. If you were that ticked off about it, why wait until months later to do anything? And murder? I mean... extreme, don't you think? And both Gianna and Amanda have said she's happy in her role as receptionist, so I'm not even sure it's an issue."

A commotion on the landing above had us swiveling our heads to watch as Gianna's body, strapped to a stretcher, was carried down the staircase. I eased my hand into Galloway's, and he gave it a comforting squeeze. Seeing Gianna, once so vibrant and full of life, now zipped into a body bag and on her way to the morgue, sucked.

I was scratching at my forehead again when I realized what was once itchy was now damp. Snatching my hand away, I examined my fingers, covered in blood. "Shoot," I whispered, patting at the pockets of my dungarees for a tissue.

"What's up?" Galloway glanced down at me, then did a double-take. "Holy heck, Audrey, you're bleeding! What did you do?"

"I was itchy!" I said defensively, trying to dab at the blood that I could now feel trickling past my temple. "It's the straw."

"Here, take it off. The hat too." Galloway teased the hat from my head, and the straw scattered on the floor around my feet, dyed bright orange but now with streaks of red. Grabbing a napkin from a table inside the ballroom, he pressed it to the self-inflicted scratch marks on my forehead.

"Is it bad?" I had a feeling it was bad. It felt bad. It felt like my forehead was on fire with a thousand burning needles.

"I'm not surprised it was itchy. I hate to tell you this, but it looks like an allergic reaction."

You have got to be kidding me! "How bad is it?" I couldn't hide the misery in my voice. Even with the offending straw gone, my skin still burned and itched.

Galloway shook his head, then dropped a kiss on

my head. "Just a red rash. And, of course, the layer of skin you took off with all the scratching. Go home and shower, maybe pop an antihistamine. I'm going to be tied up here for a while."

"Gianna was my client. I'm staying," I protested, not liking being sent home, despite being desperate to do exactly as he'd suggested.

"Babe, there's not much for you to do tonight. Crime scene processing has to be done by us."

"You're sure this isn't to get me out of the way so you can win the bet?"

"Never."

"Fine. That'll give me time to work the blackmail angle."

"You think her homicide and the blackmail are related?"

I nodded. "Hardly a coincidence that the day Gianna hires me to find her blackmailer, she's killed."

"That does put a whole new slant on things," he agreed, sliding his fingers around my nape and massaging the tense muscles in my neck. I couldn't contain the groan of appreciation. "Sorry you're going to miss out on the Scarecrow Ball," he said into my ear.

"I'm not." I sighed, leaning heavily against him. "I couldn't have gone an entire evening with the straw. We'll try again next year with different costumes."

Following Gianna's body out of the house, we stood side by side as she was loaded into a nondescript white van. Blue and red lights silently flashed, bouncing off the vehicles. Out on the street, the media waited like hungry dogs searching for a morsel to get their teeth into. A shiver raced up my spine, and goosebumps broke out on my arms.

Having felt my shudder, Galloway ran a comforting hand up and down my back. "Okay?"

"Yeah. Someone just walked over my grave."

4

I knew the moment I stepped inside the house that something was up. The Cheez-Its on the floor were a dead giveaway. I followed the trail from the front door down the hallway to the open-plan living area at the back of the house.

"Holy guacamole, what happened to you?" Ben asked, walking through the kitchen wall.

"Apparently, I'm allergic to straw." With my hands on my hips, I continued surveying the Cheez-Its-strewn floor. "Care to explain this?"

"It wasn't me!" he protested.

I snorted. "Of course it wasn't. You're incorporeal. Where have you been anyway?"

"Next door with Seb watching re-runs of *Dancing with the Stars*."

"I thought Seb was coming to the Scarecrow Ball?"

"Long story." Ben screwed up his nose.

"Mom! Mom! Mom!" Bandit smashed her way through the cat door at a million miles an hour, and the sight of her had my mouth dropping open. My raccoon no longer looked like a raccoon. She was covered in Cheez-It dust but not only that. Leaves, sticks, and something brown and sticky stuck to her fur in great chunks. I couldn't contain the eye roll.

"What have you been up to?" I asked, reluctant to give her the scratch behind the ears she was begging for until I identified whatever was stuck in her fur.

"I'm sorry, Mom." Bandit sat at my feet and looked up at me with puppy dog eyes. "I got hungry."

"You're always hungry."

"I know." She brightened. "Hey, look, Cheez-Its. My favorite." She scampered away to snatch up a nearby Cheez-It and shove it in her mouth. I mean, I couldn't blame her. My recent obsession with Cheez-Its meant the pantry was well-stocked.

My British shorthair cat, Thor, squeezed his belly through the cat door and leisurely strolled inside, his thick gray fur immaculate. *Figures.* Thor had a way of convincing Bandit to do his bidding, and Bandit, the gorgeous airhead that she is, thinks everything he suggests is the most brilliant idea on earth.

"I'm assuming this was your idea?" I asked Thor, who sat and looked at me with his orange eyes.

"You should have hidden them better." He sniffed with disdain.

"They were in the pantry. The door was shut." I glanced over at said pantry to find the door well and truly open. Shaking my head, I went to survey the damage. Raccoons were notorious trash pandas. I'd had to drill it into Bandit's head that the pantry was off-limits, but if she'd had Thor convince her it was a good idea to open the pantry door? Well, the rest, as they say, is history. Clearly, I would have to buy a bolt for the door.

"Now I know what the sticky brown stuff is," I said to myself, eyeing the open jar of peanut butter in the middle of the pantry floor. Peanut butter was smeared on the jar, on the floor, on the walls. And apparently, Bandit had rolled in it. You know, for good measure.

Ben guffawed behind me. "You know what this means?" He couldn't contain his mirth.

"Yes." I deflated like a balloon. My forehead was on fire; I dearly wanted to take a shower and get the stage makeup off my face and any remaining traces of straw from my skin. But that would have to wait.

"You need to bathe her!" Ben crowed.

"Yes," I repeated, defeated. Heaving a sigh that I felt to my very toes, I maneuvered around the mess on the floor and grabbed a bottle of olive oil, all the while listening to Ben chuckling at the predicament I found myself in. But I knew his Achilles heel. "Too bad you can't help me clean," I said, grabbing a roll of paper towel from the top shelf and shoving it under my arm. "What with having to bathe Bandit and deal with my own situation? This mess is going to have to wait until tomorrow."

"No way! You can't do that," Ben screeched.

Ben was a clean freak. And a neat freak. When he'd been alive, his home was as immaculate as any show home. Now it was my home, and I was responsible for cleaning. Leaving it in this state any longer than necessary was pure torture for him.

"You'd better get to it then," I invited, heading toward the guest bathroom. "Come on, Bandit."

"Where are we going, Mom?" Bandit happily trotted—or waddle shuffled—behind me, and I cringed at how uncomfortable she must be with her fur stuck up like that.

"We're going to a day spa!" I told her, injecting over-the-top enthusiasm into my voice. "You're going to have a beauty treatment."

"Really?" Bandit clapped her front paws together. "I love beauty treatments."

"Sure you do," Thor drawled, no doubt joining us for the amusement factor alone. I had news for him, and none of it was good.

"Sorry, Bud." I shut the bathroom door in his face. "Ladies only."

I grinned at his excessive meowing and subsequent scratching at the door.

"Thor isn't having a beauty treatment?" Bandit asked, crestfallen.

"No, sweetheart, it's just us. We're having a special date, just you and me."

Bandit perked right up. "I like special dates."

Setting the oil and paper towel on the bathroom vanity, I surveyed the bathroom, pondering my options. Bandit was too big for the hand basin. The bathtub would have to do. Turning on the tap, I adjusted the temperature and then dumped some non-soap soap in, watching as it began to froth and bubble. Bandit stood on her hind legs and peered into the bath, fascinated.

"Do I get in now?" she asked.

"Not yet." Now came the fun part. "First, we've got to get the peanut butter out of your fur. Then you get to play in the bubbles."

"I like bubbles."

"I know you do." I didn't. She'd never had a bubble bath in her life, and I never thought I'd see the day when I'd be giving her one. "I'm going to put you up on the counter here, and you're going to have to sit still while I work on your fur. Okay?"

She nodded. "Okay."

Only it wasn't okay. It was far from okay. While the olive oil removed some of the peanut butter, chunks of it had remained behind, entangled in her fur. I tried to comb it out to no avail. Which left one recourse. Bandit now sported a—let's call it edgy—fur cut.

The only saving grace in this endeavor was that Bandit didn't care. She wasn't upset that she was now missing great chunks of fur, that the fur she had left was lopsided and uneven and far from attractive. The only thing Bandit had reservations about? The bubble bath itself. Or rather being submerged in water.

Which was how Galloway found me sitting in a lukewarm bubble bath in my underwear with my raccoon. I'd taken a brief moment to wipe the makeup from my face—it turns out olive oil is an excellent makeup remover—and grabbed a clean face washer to press against the inflamed skin on my forehead. Then I'd climbed into the bath, assuring Bandit that it wasn't bottomless and she wouldn't drown.

I'd cautiously lifted her in and kept a firm hold of her as she got used to the sensation of water and bubbles, and then the little turd took to it like a duck to water.

"Dare I ask?" Galloway said, having opened the door and stuck his head inside.

"Someone whose name starts with 'Bandit' got into the pantry. Specifically, the jar of peanut butter and the Cheez-Its."

"We're having a beauty treatment!" Bandit beamed

at him. Of course, Galloway couldn't understand her. All he heard was a raccoon chittering.

"Is that right?" He humored her anyway, which is just one of the reasons I loved him. He put up with my craziness with a smile on his face and a kind heart. That made him a keeper in my book. "Is the bath nice, Bandit?" he asked her.

"I love baths!" she replied, splashing her paws in the water, sending droplets flying.

"You're back early," I said.

"Only to get changed. You're right about the straw. It is itchy."

Squatting by the side of the bath, Galloway lifted the face washer that I'd draped over my head and peered at my forehead. "That's looking better. Kinda."

"Liar." Plucking the face washer from my head, I dropped it in the water. "Here, help me with her, will you?"

Galloway grabbed a towel and held it at the ready while I picked up Bandit and passed her into his waiting arms. While he placed her on the vanity and began drying her off, I pulled the plug and climbed out of the bath, wrapping myself in a towel and maneuvering out of my sopping underwear. I caught Galloway's look.

"What?" I protested. "It felt weird getting nude and taking a bath with her."

"You know she's a raccoon, right?"

"Yeah, but you can't talk with her like I can, and the last thing I need to be doing is fielding questions about my... bits."

"What are bits?" Bandit piped in.

"Exactly my point," I deadpanned. Ruffling the damp fur on Bandit's head, I said, "Nothing for you to worry about, sweetheart. How are you feeling now? All better?"

"I like spa day!" she chortled.

I wagged my finger at her. "This does not mean you get to break into the pantry and roll in sticky things just to get a bubble bath, understood?"

Galloway lifted her off the vanity and let her loose before turning to me and wrapping me in his arms. I sank against him, suddenly exhausted from the evening's events, and it wasn't even nine o'clock yet. Smothering a yawn against his chest, I murmured, "I don't know why I'm so tired."

"I do. Your body is busy fighting off this allergic reaction. And the overall events of tonight were a lot." He dropped his voice. "Is Gianna here?"

I shook my head, yawning again. "Nah, she stayed at her place. I'll catch up with her tomorrow. I'm beat."

Resting his hands on my shoulders, he held me away from him, smiling ruefully. "You're dead on your feet. Come on, let's get you into bed. Have you taken an antihistamine yet?"

"Not yet. I had to deal with the whole Cheez-It and peanut butter fiasco first."

"Right. You run upstairs and get into bed. I'll get you an antihistamine."

I did as instructed, ignoring the mess downstairs and dragging my weary bones upstairs and into my bedroom, the towel still wrapped tightly around me. Flopping onto the bed, I was barely conscious when I heard Galloway come in. He assisted me into a sitting position to dutifully take the antihistamine before he tucked me beneath the covers with a kiss on my cheek.

I'm pretty sure he whispered, "Sweet dreams," but I can't be sure as I slipped into oblivion.

5

"*G*ood morning, Sunshine!" Seb thrust a cup of coffee into my hands, nearly blinding me with his dazzling, white smile.

"Urgh," I returned his greeting, sliding onto a barstool at my kitchen bench and taking a grateful sip of nirvana.

"I'm going to take that to mean *good morning to you too, and what are you doing in my kitchen*?" Seb wiped down the counter while carrying on the conversation for both of us. "I heard about what happened last night, came over to get the goss, but you weren't up yet, then I saw Thor and Bandit had taken liberties with your pantry, so I figured I'd be the best neighbor ever and help you out."

That's when I realized the floor was pristine, not a Cheez-It in sight.

"You're an angel, and I'll fight anyone who says otherwise," I told him, beyond grateful. While my allergic reaction had subsided, I still sported angry, self-inflicted scratches on my forehead. I felt somewhat sorry for myself when I eyed my reflection in the mirror. Knowing the mess I had waiting for me downstairs hadn't helped.

"Of course, honey." Seb patted my hand. Then I remembered Ben had said he'd been hanging out with Seb watching television last night.

"Hey, how come you didn't go to the Scarecrow Ball? Ben said you stayed in and watched *Dancing with the Stars* reruns. What's up with that?"

Seb's lips turned down at the corners. "My date canceled."

"Boo," I sympathized. "Why?"

"Dunno. I just got a text saying, *sorry, can't make it.*"

"Ouch. That sucks. Who is this guy anyway, anyone I know?"

"Myles Carter."

Chewing the inside of my cheek, I scoured my memory for anyone named Myles Carter but came up empty. "Sorry, don't know him."

Seb flicked a hand in dismissal. "Doesn't matter. It's his loss."

"Was this a first date?"

"Second. I think it's when I told him about my costume that he got cold feet."

"The whole drag queen thing?" Personally, I think Seb would look great in drag. I've seen him in shorts, and the dude has better legs than me.

Seb nodded, taking a sip of his coffee. "So, I figured I could terrorize the small-minded townsfolk of Firefly Bay and go stag or thoroughly enjoy myself with a glass of wine and *Dancing with the Stars*."

"Sound choice, considering."

Seb fluttered his hands, "Do tell, hun! What happened? And more importantly, is she here?"

Seb Castle was my new cover model gorgeous, neighbor. After catching me talking to Ben on multiple occasions, he'd quickly deduced that I could speak to the dead. And hadn't batted an eyelid. We'd cemented our friendship over the shared love of the television show *Castle*.

"She isn't here," I said. "And her name is Gianna Tate."

"Is it true she's a lawyer?"

I nodded. "Uh-huh. And she doesn't know she's dead."

"Who doesn't?" Ben appeared, making me jump.

"Gianna Tate, the woman killed last night," I replied, and then to Seb, "Ben's here."

"Hey, Ben!" Seb greeted.

"Tell him hi," Ben said.

"He says hi," I repeated. "Ben, have you seen Gianna around? She's still in her fancy dress costume, like Cinderella, but she's actually the Fairy Godmother. Can't miss her—stab wound to the abdomen."

Ben shook his head. "Nope, but I can go looking for her if you want?"

"I need your help with something else first."

"Oh?"

"Gianna said she'd been about to hire me to find out who was behind a blackmail attempt on her. Apparently, someone has some risqué photos from her youth that they threatened to make public. She wanted anything incriminating gone."

"Any ideas who?"

"Nope." I shook my head. "But I want to see those emails, which means I need to get into her office, and I could use your help with her computer." Ben had this neat trick where he could touch a computer or phone and read through all the digital data.

"Sure. But have you remembered it's Sunday? How are you going to get into her office?"

"Good thing I have a sister-in-law who works there, isn't it?"

———

It took some fast talking, but I eventually convinced Amanda to meet me at the Beasley, Tate, and Associates offices an hour later.

"God, Audrey, your face!" she'd exclaimed when she saw me waiting at the front door.

"That's just rude, Amanda," I shot back, although, truth be told, I wasn't insulted. Anything that came out of Amanda's mouth was to be expected. And to be fair, the angry red scratches looked alarming.

"Sorry. I didn't mean..." she cleared her throat. "What I meant to say is, that looks—"

"Nasty? Gross?"

"Painful."

"Yeah, well, turns out I'm allergic to straw. Or the dye that was used to color the straw. Of course, I wasn't aware of that when I shoved a bunch of it under my hat." I cocked a thumb toward the locked doors. "Shall we?"

Using her key, Amanda unlocked the door and preceded me inside, punching a code into the alarm keypad. "I'm not sure I should be letting you do this," she said, chewing at her bottom lip.

"It's fine. If I find anything incriminating, I'll let the police know." I waved away her concerns. Plus, I had no intentions of telling anyone she'd given me access to the offices. I didn't want to get her—or myself—in trouble.

Amanda gave a nod, then led the way to Gianna's office.

"Wow. Nice." I stepped inside, the carpet plush beneath my feet. Her office was huge, dominated by a large desk with two barrel chairs in front of it, a wall with floor-to-ceiling bookcases that held what I assumed to be law books, some of them leather-bound. What I hadn't been expecting was Gianna herself to be seated behind the desk.

"Oh good, you're here," she said, glancing up from her computer where she appeared to be typing. Only the keys weren't clacking, and I wasn't sure her computer was even turned on. She finished typing and stood. "Perfect timing."

What was even more startling than Gianna being in her office apparently working, was her clothing. Gone was the ball gown costume. In its place was what I assumed to be her usual office attire. I wondered if she had a stylist and, if so, who. The mustard-colored tunic with the rusty red Capris was amazeballs. No stuffy suit for her. No pearls either. Around her neck was a chunky gold link necklace. She sported rings on every finger, a huge white watch on her left wrist, and three gold bracelets that matched the necklace on her right. I looked down at the diamond sparkling on my left hand and smiled. My engagement ring was more than enough jewelry for me.

"Sit, sit." Gianna waved at one of the chairs situated in front of her desk. "That'll be all, Amanda."

I quickly turned to my sister-in-law. "Thanks, Amanda. If you wouldn't mind?" I gestured toward the door, indicating she could leave.

"I'm not sure I should leave you here alone." She chewed her lip some more, and I glanced toward Gianna, who was thankfully ignoring our exchange.

"How about you get us a coffee?" I suggested buying some time. It wouldn't take Ben long to do his thing on the computer, and then we could be out of here. Ben had followed me in and, for once, was remaining blessedly silent.

"I guess that'd be okay." She left, leaving the door ajar.

"Why are you still standing over there?" Gianna snapped. "Sit."

Lowering myself into the barrel chair opposite her desk, I realized immediately that I'd made a colossal mistake. While appearing sturdy, solid, and comfortable, the chair was deceptive. I sank into the cushions so deep I doubted I'd be able to get out again.

"Thank you so much for agreeing to this," Gianna said, not noticing my predicament. Nor Ben's presence. I looked at my best friend, who returned my look with a raised brow.

"Thanks for hiring me." I smiled, trying to cross my legs, only the ass-eating chair prevented it.

"So... how does this work?" Gianna came around to my side of the desk, leaning against it, looking down at me. I don't like being looked down on, even by someone as beautiful and powerful as Gianna Tate. I think better when I walk, so I decided to abandon the chair and stand. I struggled for a solid minute—which felt like thirty—trying to get out of the plush chair before admitting defeat and holding out a hand to Gianna. "Here," I puffed, working up a sweat. "Give a girl a hand, would you?"

Only, of course, she couldn't. Because she was a ghost. She seemed genuinely puzzled when she couldn't grasp my hand. I could have smacked myself in the forehead for forgetting, for the briefest of moments, that she was incorporeal and was of zero help getting me out of the chair. Instead, I had to resort to lowering my torso to my thighs and flinging myself forward. I landed on my hands and knees on the floor before using the edge of the desk to haul myself to my feet.

Dusting myself off, I glared at the chair. "No offense, but those chairs? Terrible. They eat your ass."

Gianna blinked, staring at me in silence, before tilting her head back and roaring with laughter.

"Thank you for your candor," she chortled. "No one has ever told me that before."

I bet. When you were paying the type of fees Gianna commanded, you wouldn't dare insult her furniture.

"You told me earlier that you're being blackmailed?" I straightened my T-shirt and smoothed my palms down my denim-clad thighs. "Would you mind if we took a look at your computer?" I waved a hand toward the item in question, knocking over a photo frame on Gianna's desk. Quickly righting it, I muttered an apology which Gianna waved away.

"It's probably better if I show you," Gianna said, retreating behind her desk. Rather than taking a seat, she leaned over her keyboard and quickly typed in her password, oblivious that the computer wasn't on and she wasn't actually typing. "Here. Sit."

I slid into her white office chair, gasping at the ergonomic delight that it was. Gianna grinned. "Comfy, eh?"

I ran my hands up and down the arms. "This chair? This chair is a dream!" I declared. I needed one for my home office. "How much is it?"

"Hmmm." Gianna tapped a manicured nail against her chin. "I think this one was around two thousand."

Okay. Maybe I'd make do with Ben's old office chair after all. Turning my attention to the computer, I turned it on and waited for it to boot up. "Ummm, have you met Ben?" I pointed toward the ghost of Ben Delaney, the previous owner of Delaney Investigations and my best friend.

"Who?" Gianna frowned, not even glancing Ben's way. Could she not see him? This was all very odd.

"Ben's a work colleague," I explained. Leaning forward and placing my fingers on the keyboard, I asked, "Password?"

I wasn't expecting her to tell me. I was preparing to

wait it out while she attempted to type it in herself, but nope, she merely rattled off what seemed to be a random collection of numbers and letters that I was secretly impressed she'd managed to memorize.

Once we were in, I pulled up her emails.

"Here." Gianna pointed to the monitor. "Read this email. I'm sorry, I know it would have been easier if I simply forwarded it to you, but I can't risk this sort of thing leaking."

"I get it," I assured her. "You want to keep it under wraps." Of course, now that she'd been murdered, the police would be all over this, but hey, if I could get a head start, maybe I could catch the killer before Galloway.

Leaning forward, I read the email. The address it was sent from was obviously bogus, a bunch of random letters and numbers from a Gmail address. In the body of the email were vague threats about some risqué photos from her youth, just like she'd said.

"I asked you this before, but have you had time to think back? Are there risqué photos from your youth?" I asked.

Gianna smirked. "If we're talking college days, then maybe? I got up to some pretty wild stuff back then. If someone took photos of me naked," she winked, "I'm not aware of it. Cell phone cameras didn't exist back then. Heck, cell phones barely existed."

I stole a glance at her out of the corner of my eye. It

was hard to imagine this immaculately groomed and incredibly well-styled woman having a sordid past, but then we were all young once, and there are one or two episodes in my past that I wouldn't want any photos of floating around. Not nudes or anything of that nature. More like embarrassing mishaps that had me looking like a fool.

"Ordinarily, I wouldn't pay this type of nonsense any heed," Gianna continued, moving around to the opposite side of the desk and leaving me sitting in her chair. She took a seat on one of the guest chairs and gasped. "Oh my God! You're right! These are appalling." Then she burst into laughter, and I couldn't help but join in before quickly sobering in case Amanda heard me.

"Let me see if I can find the IP address this was sent from," I said, jerking my head toward Ben, who obligingly stepped forward and placed his hand on top of the computer. The screen fritzed and filled with static.

"While we wait, is there anyone you were having a problem with? Disgruntled client? Employees?"

Gianna shook her head. "No, nothing like that. Which is why I hired you."

"Right. And yesterday? What were your movements yesterday?"

"It's all there in my planner." Gianna waved a hand at the computer, and I looked at Ben.

"Can you send me a copy of the email and her planner?" I whispered under my breath.

"Sure."

"Why don't you tell me anyway?" I said to Gianna.

Gianna frowned, rubbing at her brow. "What day was yesterday?"

I looked at Ben, then back at Gianna. "Saturday. Yesterday was Saturday. And last night was the Scarecrow Ball. Remember?"

Her face cleared, and she smiled. "Oh, yes! The ball. I had a wonderful time. Were you there? Did you enjoy yourself?"

"Oh, erm, I developed an allergic reaction and had to leave early," I quickly said, taken aback once again by her lack of self-awareness that she was, in fact, dead.

"She is so deeply ingrained in denial that she thinks she's still alive," Ben said. I waited for Gianna to call him out on it, but it was like he hadn't spoken. Like she had no clue he was there.

"You're right," I said to him.

"Who are you talking to?" Gianna asked. Before I could answer, Amanda pushed the door open, carrying two cups of coffee. "Sorry it took so long. I had to wait for the water to boil," Amanda said.

"No problem. I'm just checking Gianna's planner."

"You're not accessing client files, are you?" Amanda hurried around the desk to peer over my shoulder, frowning at the static on the monitor.

"Nope."

"That's odd." She thwacked the side of the monitor a couple of times, and Ben grinned at her, his hand still half in, half out, of the computer as he did his thing.

"I figured it's just warming up." I shrugged, hoping Ben would hurry up before Amanda accused me of breaking it. I'd no sooner thought it than he lifted his hand. The screen sharpened into focus, the cursor flashing, waiting for Gianna's password.

"You're welcome." Ben grinned.

"Thank you," I mouthed, knowing Amanda would have questions if she'd seen I'd already been into Gianna's emails and calendar.

I glanced across at Gianna, wondering what she'd make of all this, but Gianna was over by a filing cabinet, apparently engrossed in... something? She must have sensed me looking at her, for she waved a hand in my direction without looking up. "Don't mind me. You keep doing what you're doing. I'm prepping for court tomorrow."

"When it finally hits her," Ben said, "it will hit hard."

It was with an overwhelming sense of sadness that I had to agree.

6

I went through Gianna's emails and calendar with Amanda hovering over my shoulder. Ben had hidden the blackmail threat, meaning there was nothing for Amanda to find, which saved me from lying to her. Because if Amanda knew, she'd be bound to tell her work colleagues, especially Felix, and I didn't want to tip the blackmailer off that we were on to them.

"This twelve o'clock lunch at the Bay yesterday." I tapped the monitor. "Do you know who that was with? There's no name."

Amanda shrugged. "I'd assume it's personal. Why? Do you think it's relevant?"

I'd hoped Gianna would chime in, but she was engrossed in her *work* and totally oblivious to us. Ben had wandered over to her to try and get her attention, but she acted as if she couldn't see or hear him. Maybe she couldn't. I honestly didn't know what to think anymore.

"Not necessarily." I leaned back in the chair before reluctantly standing. "I think I've got all I can from this." I nodded toward Gianna's calendar. "What about Gianna's current cases—would anyone benefit from her demise?"

"Let me see…" Amanda nudged me out of the way and took the coveted seat while I finished my coffee and watched on. Her fingers flew across the keyboard as she brought up Gianna's case files.

"She was working on the Harris's divorce."

"Anything unusual about it? Was it acrimonious?"

Amanda was speed reading the file. "Gianna was representing June Harris in a divorce from her husband, Adam. They'd been in mediation and unable to come to a settlement. The court case is tomorrow."

"Will that still go ahead with Gianna unable to represent Mrs. Harris?"

"Jack will probably take it on."

"Oh." Darn, there went that motive.

"Plus, the settlement they're wrangling over? Hardly worthy of murder," Amanda said drolly, drawing my attention to a paragraph on the screen.

"A dog?"

"Mmmhmm. They both want custody of the dog.

They couldn't reach an amicable arrangement. This is why it's going to court."

"And Gianna took the case? Wouldn't that be something she'd hand down to one of the other attorneys?" Why would a high-powered professional like Gianna take such a case?

Amanda scratched her head. "She is an animal lover. Maybe that's why she took it."

I looked across the room to Gianna, making a mental note to ask her directly once we were alone.

"Okay, thanks for this, but I should get going," I said.

"No problem." I watched while Amanda turned off the computer and picked up the empty coffee cups. "I hope that doesn't scar."

"What?"

She jerked her head toward my forehead. "Those scratches. I hope they don't scar. But I guess your veil will hide it."

"My veil?" What on earth was she talking about?

"Yes. Your veil. Wedding veil. Your mom said the two of you are going wedding dress shopping this week. If you let me know what time, I'll take time off and come with."

"Oh." I shook my head. "I'm not wearing a veil." And heaven forbid having Amanda in on my wedding dress choices. She'd have me strapped in with a collar up to my neck and sleeves to my wrists.

"You have to wear a veil!" she protested vehemently. "It's tradition."

"Whose?" I snorted. Amanda should know by now not to argue with me. As soon as she said something should be one way, I'd automatically argue the opposite. And dig my heels in to boot.

"Please tell me you're at least wearing white," she groaned, leading the way out of Gianna's office.

"Actually... I was thinking purple?" I wasn't. Not specifically. But I also *wasn't* thinking white.

The coffee cups clattered to the carpet with a thud, thankfully not broken, and Amanda spun to stare at me, aghast.

"Uh oh!" Ben drawled. "Bridezilla alert."

"You are what?" Amanda screeched.

I glanced at my wrist where I wasn't wearing a watch and declared, "Is that the time? I've gotta run." I bolted out of the Beasley, Tate, and Associates offices before Amanda could waylay me further and demand I reconsider my wedding dress choices. Which I hadn't even decided on yet. But it had been fun to pull her chain.

"Is purple really a color choice?" Ben asked from the passenger seat after I'd slid behind the wheel. "Maybe. Could be. I really don't know—I haven't decided. One thing I do know is that my dress won't be white." I held out a pale arm. "See this skin tone? I'm white enough as it is. I mean, I could probably get away with an ivory or cream, but seriously, is it so wrong to want to get married in a dress that isn't white?"

Ben shook his head. "Not at all. You'll look fabulous no matter what you wear."

"Correct answer." I grinned at my BFF. Shoving the car into reverse, I maneuvered out of the parking space and headed west. "Where are we going?" I belatedly asked.

"I traced the IP to the Firefly Bay Public Library," Ben said, pointing through the windshield.

I smacked my lips together. "Smart. Use a public computer. When was the email sent?"

"Thursday at twelve-seventeen."

"Lunchtime. So, anyone could have ducked in on their lunch break and fired off the email," I surmised.

"Affirmative."

I pulled into the free parking lot off Atlantic Avenue and scored a park close to the library's doors two minutes later. Should have realized it was too good to be true. "Looks like it's closed," Ben said.

I followed his gaze to the glass doors and the darkness within. "Looks like. Could you still do your thing?"

"My thing?"

"Yeah, you know. Your thing." I wriggled my fingers in the air. "Your technology magicy thing. Does it even work if the computers aren't turned on?"

"Lemme try. Wait here."

He disappeared. Spotting the crumpled box of Cheez-Its from the night before, I rummaged inside, smiling when my fingers closed around a fistful of the cheesy delights.

"Urgh," I mumbled, mouth full. "Thethe are thstale." But I chewed anyway cos Cheez-Its are Cheez-Its, and beggars can't be choosers. And, of course, with my mouth full of stale Cheez-Its, my phone rang. Naturally. Because when else would it ring? Dusting off my fingers, I squinted at the screen. Mom calling.

"'lo?" I answered.

"Are you eating?" Mom demanded.

I finished chewing and swallowed. "No."

"Anyway, Amanda called. She was hysterical. She said you're getting married in purple."

I'm glad I'd finished the mouthful of Cheez-Its, for surely, I would have choked. "Relax, Mom, I'm not getting married in purple. At least, I don't think I am. Unless they have a knock-out purple wedding dress in the store, in which case, I just might."

The silence that followed stretched on for so long that I thought we'd been disconnected. "Hello? You still there?" I looked at the screen to check.

Mom cleared her throat. "I'm here. But you are joking, right?"

I expelled a loud breath. "Mom, I promise, whatever I choose will be beautiful and bridey, but prepare yourself for the possibility that it may not be white. White really isn't my color." Not to mention the spill factor. Have you met me? I trip over nothing and choke on air. Wearing white would not be the wisest of choices.

"You are very pale," she agreed. "An ivory, perhaps?"

"Or even mocha. Blush pink. Something pastel. Or not."

"Well, I guess that wouldn't be so bad," she conceded.

"Oh, and I'll tell you what I told Amanda. No veil. I'm not the veil-wearing type. I think I'd prefer flowers or a tiara to a veil." Or, you know, nothing at all.

"You'd look lovely wearing a tiara." Mom sighed, her mind already picturing me walking down the aisle.

"Or a crown," I teased, and Mom laughed. With all the planning and stressing she was doing, you'd think it was her wedding. But I was the last of her babies to get married, and I knew she only wanted the best for me. Laura had done the white dress and veil thing, complete with church and half a dozen bridesmaids. That wasn't my style. Dustin and Amanda's shindig had been worthy of a royal wedding, and I remember my discomfort in the yellow tulle bridesmaid ballgown I'd been forced to endure. Galloway and I would get married barefoot on the beach, preferably in jeans, if I had my way. That I was even contemplating a dress was a huge concession on my part.

"Where are you, anyway? Amanda said you're working Gianna's case?"

"I'm at the library."

"The library. But it's closed on Sundays."

"So I discovered. Look, Ma, I gotta run. I'll see you later, okay?"

"Okay, sweetheart. Love you."

"Love you too, Mom. Bye."

Ben returned moments later, shaking his head. "No can do. Everything is powered down. I'll have to come back tomorrow."

"Thanks for trying."

"What are we going to do now?"

"What we should have done hours ago."

"What's that?"

"Grab a beer."

Leaning across the bar, I held my phone toward the burly bartender I wouldn't want to take on in close quarters. I could probably outrun him, though.

"Have you seen this woman? Say about this time yesterday?"

For a Sunday, The Bay was hopping, country music blaring, clientele of all shapes and ages chasing away the residual hangover from the night before or working on a new one.

"Yeah, I remember her. She got into an argument with her friend and the guy split."

"Got a name for her friend? Credit card receipt?"

"Nope. Paid cash."

"What were they fighting about?"

"Don't know, but after he'd left, she got into an argument with someone else." My brows rose, causing the healing scabs of my scratches to pull. The bartender's eyes drifted to my self-inflicted injury. "Catfight?" he asked, a gleam of interest sparking in his eyes.

You wish, buddy. It wouldn't be the worst or strangest I'd ever heard as far as stories went. Sounded way better than an allergic reaction to colored straw.

"Got a description of that guy?" I asked instead.

"Kinda scrawny. Scar over his right eye."

I glanced at Ben, leaning next to me, his back against the bar as he surveyed the room.

"Some sort of bike club," he said.

"What?"

"This crowd. Some sort of bike club. Didn't you notice all the motorcycles out front? They're obviously out for a cruise and stopped here for lunch."

"Yeah? So?" I looked over my shoulder at the leather-clad riders. If I'd been drinking, I would have spit it out, for before me were the oldest bikers I'd ever seen. And they were women. What was this, the granny gray nomads? I cocked my head, wondering if I was too young to join.

"Look, are you going to order or not?" the bartender groused. "Cos I'm kinda busy here."

"I'll take a cider." He gave a nod and spun away to grab my drink.

"Ben, can you check the CCTV? See who Gianna was here with yesterday?"

Ben followed my line of sight where I'd spotted a camera mounted in the corner, aimed toward the bar.

"Now that, I can do."

It didn't take long. Ben popped up from behind the bar just as the bartender returned with my cider. He walked right through Ben, shivering as he did so.

"Urgh," he grumbled. "Someone just walked over my grave." I tried to keep my face neutral and probably failed, judging by the puzzled look he gave me, but honestly, watching him walk through Ben? It gave me the heebie-jeebies and made me shudder in sympathy.

"Ummm, thanks." I shoved a handful of bills toward him. He snatched them up, muttering under his breath about lousy tippers as he hurried away to serve someone else.

Ben was laughing and shaking his head at me.

"What?" I protested.

"You are as transparent as a sheet of glass," he chortled.

"What are you even talking about?" Then I realized I was talking to him with no props to disguise that I was talking to thin air. Snatching my phone to my ear, I pretended to take a call. "What is so funny?" I demanded.

"Your face, when he walked through me!" Ben was about doubled over with mirth.

I waited a full twenty seconds. "Have you quite finished?"

He held up a hand, dragging in an exaggerated breath. "Almost."

"Did you find anything? On the CCTV?"

He sobered. "Yeah, put your phone down, far enough over so I can reach it and the camera receiver simultaneously, and I'll see if I can forward you a still capture."

"You can do that?" How cool. Ben was proving to be an invaluable sleuthing tool.

"I can try." Ben laid one hand on my phone, and with the other, he reached beneath the bar, stretching. "Can't quite reach. Nudge it over a bit."

I did as instructed, shuffling over and bumping my phone so it slid a few inches along the bar.

"Perfect. There. Done. Did it work?"

I picked up my phone and there, in my camera roll, was a new photo. One I didn't take. It showed Gianna and a man seated on the sofa on the far side of the room. Gianna was leaning back, appearing relaxed.

The man sitting opposite her leaned forward, elbows on knees, hands gesturing, face intent.

"Did you see the argument?" I asked Ben, studying the still shot he'd sent me.

"Yeah. It happened just after this. The guy was clearly worked up, arms waving. Gianna just sat there, shrugged her shoulders, and shook her head. He stormed out."

"And what about the other argument? The bartender said as soon as her friend left, she got into another fight?"

"Yeah. There should be another photo."

I flicked through to the next photo. Sure enough, a scrawny guy with a scar above one eye was yelling at Gianna. Other patrons were physically restraining him. "It looks intense."

"He was yelling that he would kill her, that she ruined his life, and he'd make her pay. He was also very intoxicated," Ben said.

"Do you recognize either of these men?"

He shook his head. "Nope. The best person to ask would be Gianna."

"She's probably still at her office. But it's Sunday, and the office is locked," I pointed out. "I already had Amanda let me in this morning. I don't want to bother her again."

"Are you forgetting I'm a ghost?"

"How could I possibly forget that?" *Duh.*

"What I'm getting at is that we don't need Amanda to get into Gianna's office. You know how to pick a lock, and I watched Amanda type in the alarm code this morning."

My mouth dropped open, and my eyes rounded. "Are you suggesting we break and enter?" My face relaxed, and I grinned. "I like it."

7

"*N*o," Galloway said into my ear, making me jump. I'd paused in front of The Bay to admire the line of motorcycles parked outside, chrome exhausts sparkling in the sun.

"What?" I protested, fluttering my eyelashes and eyeing him up and down.

"No. You cannot have a motorcycle with your coordination," he replied, mouth quirking in that sexy smile he did so well.

"Awww, but Mom!" I teased, and he laughed.

"Find out anything?" he cocked his head toward the bar.

"A guy with a scar over his eye was threatening to kill her all afternoon." I held out my phone to show him the photo, forgetting that we were in competition.

"Do I want to know how you got that?"

"No?" I fluttered my eyelashes again, and he sighed, kissing my forehead.

"CCTV?" he guessed.

"Affirmative. Courtesy of Ben."

"Anything else?"

"Yeah, she was lunching with a friend who left in a huff. Do you know this guy?" I flicked to the next photo on my phone.

Galloway took it from me and squinted at the screen. "I've seen him before."

"He's a crim?" My heart rate shot up as a burst of adrenaline surged through me. If Gianna was being threatened by a known criminal, we could, potentially, have our killer. Or maybe our blackmailer. Or both!

Galloway dashed my hopes when he shook his head. "Nah. I think he's a personal trainer. I've seen his picture on a flyer pinned to the notice board at work. He's offering law enforcement a deal for sessions at his gym."

"Oh."

Galloway laughed. "Try not to look so disappointed. Which reminds me, preliminary autopsy results are in. Gianna Tate was stabbed." Dropping a soft kiss on my lips, he cupped my face, and I swear to God I practically melted into a puddle at his feet. "I'll see you back at your place tonight?" he murmured against my mouth.

"You bet. We can compare notes. Be prepared to

lose." I patted his denim-clad rear and winked, making him laugh.

"Game on, Fitz." I enjoyed watching him walk away until Ben elbowed me in the ribs, sending a shard of freezing air into my internal organs.

"Quit ogling your fiancé," he teased, "and get your mind back in the game. If you want to beat Galloway in solving this case, you've got to stay one step ahead. And in case you didn't notice, he just gave you a lead."

"Right. The gym." I snapped out of it. "Let's go."

"And hold it, breathe." A man in his late forties wearing track pants and a tank top stood over a trim young woman in the downward dog pose, butt in the air.

"Nice," I said sarcastically, not missing how the trainer's eyes lingered on the woman's curves. "Harry Watts?" It hadn't taken us long to find the gym once Galloway had given us the lead. Ben had simply zapped himself to the police station and read the flyer.

"Later," Watts snapped. "Can't you see I'm with a client?"

"I can see you're putting this woman into uncomfortable positions so you can stare at her butt." I held out my business card. "Audrey Fitzgerald, PI."

Harry Watts snatched the card from my fingers and

glared at it as if he wished hard enough it would burst into flames. To his client, he said, "Take five, babe." She relaxed onto all fours, then stood, grabbed her towel and water bottle, and walked away. "Make sure you hydrate," Watts called after her, then rounded on me, his breath hot on my face. "What do you want?"

"Well, for starters, Popeye, you can take your tone down a notch. And a mint wouldn't hurt." I wiped a finger across my cheek, removing the damp mist of his breath from my skin. Later, I'd go home and disinfect my face, but right now, I kept my expression neutral, hiding my revulsion.

"Pretty smart mouth for a girl I can snap in two. Did you bring backup?"

I smiled sweetly. "Nope. Just me." If he was hoping to intimidate me, he was all out of luck. Not only did I have Ben, who admittedly had drifted after Watts's client and wasn't paying a whole lot of attention to our altercation, but there were other people in the gym. I figured Watts wasn't stupid enough to try anything here. But then again, if the guy was beefed up on 'roids, anything could happen.

"What the hell do you want?" He stepped back.

"I understand Gianna Tate was a client of yours?" It was a guess. Ben was supposed to be checking the records, but instead, he was busy drooling over Miss Universe in her Lululemon leggings. I figured Gianna probably had a personal trainer, given her trim physique. It would be so helpful if she woke up and realized she was a ghost—then I wouldn't have to do all this running around!

"What of it?"

"I also understand the two of you got into a fight at The Bay yesterday."

"Wasn't a fight." He crossed his beefy arms across his chest and frowned at me.

I cocked my head. "You do know she's been murdered, right?"

His arms dropped to his sides, and his face fell slack in a combination of shock and horror. "I didn't hear from her, so I figured she'd quit training."

"Is that what the fight was about? Her quitting training?"

"Told you, it wasn't a fight."

"A *discussion* then."

He remained tight-lipped. A vein in his neck throbbed. It was rather distracting. As was the clench of his jaw.

Time to change tacks. "Word is Gianna is cold-hearted and a bulldog in court."

"Yeah, well, they don't know her like I do. We grew up on the same street. She was like a sister to me."

"Well, what did you two siblings fight about the day she was murdered?" I pressed.

Harry Watts squared his shoulders. "She was drinking too much. I told her to stop. She wouldn't."

"You were mad she was spending her money on booze rather than a PT session with you? I mean, a woman of Gianna's wealth, how many sessions was she having with you a week? Four? Five? Seems to me like she was your meal ticket."

"Look, I scratch her back; she scratches mine," Watts scoffed. "If I train a client who is unhappy in her marriage, I send her Gianna's way."

"And what's in it for you?"

"I want to open my own gym, and Gianna was going to co-sign the loan, so you tell me, smart mouth." Watts poked me in the shoulder. "Why would I kill her?"

Why indeed? As far as motives go, he had none. Unless he was the blackmailer. But she was going to co-sign the loan. He didn't need to extort money out of her. And killing her would be killing his dreams, which I could see he'd just realized were dashed.

"Where were you at seven last night?"

"With a client." Throwing my business card to the ground, he stomped off, seemingly forgetting he was in the middle of a PT session with a client.

"That seemed to go well." Ben caught up with me as I headed outside.

I gave him the side-eye. "I'm surprised you even noticed."

Ben ignored my dig. "Well? What did he say?"

"He said that she'd missed some training sessions and drank too much."

"And *that's* what they fought about?"

"I didn't believe it either. But he also said Gianna had agreed to co-sign a loan for him to set up his own gym."

"Ah." Ben held up a finger. "No motive for murder. It was in his best interests to keep her alive."

"Exactly. Unless she reneged on the deal?"

"One way to find out," Ben said.

I nodded. "We need to go talk to her."

Ben rubbed his hands together in delight. "The B&E is back on!"

We headed back to Beasley, Tate, and Associates with Ben riding shotgun. Amanda had left, and the building was shut, the lights off. Grabbing my lock picking gear from the glovebox, I headed toward the front door.

"Keep an eye out, will you?" I said to Ben, overly aware that I was brazenly breaking into an office building in broad daylight. This was the difference between Galloway's job and mine. I could gain information via unconventional methods while Galloway had to wait around for a warrant.

"I'm so glad you left the force and became a private investigator," I said to Ben while maneuvering the pick in the lock, feeling for the tumblers and grinning in triumph when they clicked down, unlocking the door.

Ben's smile was a little melancholy as he stepped through the door and stood by the alarm keypad waiting for me to join him. "Yeah, well, it wasn't by choice, but it all worked out for the best."

Sliding inside, I locked the door behind me and punched in the number Ben relayed to me. The alarm disarmed before blaring out to all and sundry that we'd broken in.

"All except for the last part," I said softly, eyes going misty. I missed him. I missed him being alive. His murder had been the hardest thing I'd ever lived through.

"Hey, now." Ben slapped my back, which in turn made my shoulders snap backward at the cold jolt his touch brought. "Don't go getting maudlin on me. Of course, I'd prefer to be alive, but if being in this form means I still get to hang with you, then I'm good with it."

"You'll tell me, though, won't you? If that ever changes and you want to move on?"

"Quit worrying, Fitz. I'm not going anywhere. Now get your butt out of the foyer. There's a car coming, and if they happen to glance over and see someone standing here, they might call the cops."

I scooted behind the reception desk and ducked, waiting until the car had passed before peeking over the top. Once the coast was clear, I stood to my full height and headed deeper into the building and down the corridor toward Gianna's plush office. Pushing her door open, I stepped inside.

"Oh, good, you're back." Gianna glanced up from where she had dozens of files spread open across her desk. I didn't know how she managed it until I took a closer look and realized the files were like Gianna. Incorporeal.

"This is the weirdest case ever," I said to Ben.

"Who's this?" Gianna's eyes locked on Ben, one brow arched.

"You can see him?" I gasped.

"Of course, I can see him. What sort of question is that?"

"Yes, right. Of course." I cleared my throat. "Gianna, this is my dear friend Ben Delaney. Ben, Gianna Tate."

Ben inclined his head. "Pleasure."

Gianna cocked her head, studying him intently. "You look familiar. Do I know you?"

He shook his head. "Doubtful, unless our paths crossed when I was on the force."

"You're a police officer?"

"Was. I left to start my own PI business."

She snapped her fingers. "Delaney Investigations! So, you're Audrey's boss?"

I snorted out a laugh. "Hardly."

"Audrey has taken over the business," Ben corrected.

"Oh. So you're here on a consultancy basis?"

Ben glanced at me, and I shrugged. "You could say that, I suppose."

Gianna nodded. "Good, good." She picked up a file and began leafing through the pages.

"How is she doing that?" I whispered to Ben.

"They're not real," he whispered back.

"But how did she... make them?"

Gianna tossed the file onto the desk and pinned us both with a stern look. "I can hear you, you know."

"Sorry."

"I don't want apologies. I want you to find whoever is behind this blackmail attempt." She pointed to the file on her desk. "And who killed me."

8

*B*en picked up the file. "This is great. How did you do it?"

"What? Make a file? Pretty basic, I would have thought," Gianna snapped, her nostrils flaring.

Ben gave her a look. One that said he didn't appreciate her tone. "I meant since you are a *ghost*," he emphasized the word, "how did you create an incorporeal object? Usually, that isn't something we can do."

"Ghost?" she repeated, and I shot a worried look at Ben. Was she about to lose it? Freak out because she'd discovered the truth?

"Correct."

Then Gianna laughed. "Oh my gosh, but I feel like an idiot. All this time, I've been running around dead."

She looked at me. "Why didn't you say anything? I must say, you handled yourself remarkably well."

"You were in denial, and initially, when you couldn't see Ben? I didn't know what to make of the whole situation, so I thought I'd let it play out. When did you figure it out?"

"When I saw my murder on the news."

I glanced toward the flat-screen television affixed to Gianna's wall, the screen black. How could she have watched the news when the TV wasn't on?

Gianna saw my confusion. "I went to grab a coffee from the café down the street. Only I couldn't get them to serve me, and they have a television behind the counter. While I was waiting, the news came on. My murder was the top story."

"I'm sorry." I was. Finding out you were dead had to suck. Finding out so long after the fact had to doubly suck.

"So?" she demanded, hands-on-hips. "Tell me what you've discovered."

I exchanged another look with Ben. "Do you remember what happened?" he asked instead.

She looked at him blankly. "What?"

"The night you died," he prompted. "Do you remember what happened? The fastest way to solve a murder is to ask the victim who did it."

Her mouth opened and closed a couple of times, and I could practically see the cogs turning as she searched her memory for answers. "We were at the pre-party at my house," she began, squinting her eyes as if she'd find the answer through pinpoint vision.

"Who was there?" Ben asked.

"All the staff from Beasley, Tate, and Associates. Plus the catering staff. Three in total. It's just a small affair but opulent, to let the team know how much we appreciate them."

"Did anyone turn up that you weren't expecting?" I asked.

She shook her head. "No."

"Do you remember going upstairs? To your bedroom?"

She frowned. "I think so." Her hand went to her throat. "My necklace broke. I went upstairs to put it in my jewelry box, thinking I'd send it to the jeweler during the week to be repaired."

"Who did you see in your dressing room?" Ben asked.

"No one. There was no one there. I had the necklace in my hand. I put it into the wooden jewelry box I keep in the top drawer of the island bench in my dressing room. I closed the drawer and left."

Only she hadn't. Sometime between closing the drawer and leaving, she was killed.

A look I'd never seen before splashed across her face. Panic. "Why can't I remember?" she cried.

Ben put a gentle hand on her arm. "It's okay. This

happens a lot. Sometimes, when you die suddenly and violently, you don't retain that memory."

She sucked in a shuddering breath. "Did that happen to you?"

He nodded. "Yeah. But Audrey figured it out. She caught my killer. And she'll find yours too."

"I'll do my best," I said with a firm nod.

Gianna ran her hands over her face, sucked in another breath, and squared her shoulders. "Right. Pulling myself together." She blew out her breath. "You came here for a reason. To ask me something?"

"Yes. Harry Watts. You had lunch with him yesterday at The Bay, and the two of you got into a disagreement. Do you remember?"

Gianna smiled warmly. "Ah yes, Harry. We grew up together, neighbors in fact."

"Is that so," Ben drawled. I looked at him, and he shrugged, and I wasn't sure if he was trying to tell me something or not. Harry had already told us they'd grown up on the same street.

"He also said you were arguing because he was concerned with your drinking," Ben said.

"What?" Her screech was ear-splitting, and I winced, covering my ears with my hands. "That little —" She cut herself off, but I could guess what she'd been going to say.

"Liar?" I suggested.

She began pacing. "Yes. Liar just about covers it."

She paced and shook her head at the same time. "I tried to help him. I really did."

"By co-signing a loan so he could open his own gym," I prompted.

She looked at me but didn't stop pacing. "I was going to. And then I saw his business plan."

"Not good?" Ben guessed.

"It was rubbish. It was like he'd plucked numbers out of his—" She caught herself and corrected. "Thin air—with nothing to back them up. Of course, I called him out on it. If I'm going to invest in his business, he'd better damn sure make a success of it, and he wasn't off to a good start." She paced and ranted, then ranted some more. "Originally, he didn't even have a business plan. Not until I asked him for it and told him the bank would ask for it too. It's not like buying a car. You need market research and a clear plan on how you're going to market it, how you're going to repay the loan and other creditors."

"So, you withdrew the offer to co-sign the loan," Ben stated, crossing his arms over his chest.

Gianna paused. "Actually, no."

"No?"

She shook her head. "I wanted him to be successful. And to be successful, he needed to do things right, which meant having the right people around him advising him. I gave him free business advice, recommended an accountant and a financial advisor, and told him to start over with the business plan. I wasn't signing anything until he could develop a document that made good business sense."

"But overall, you think the gym idea was solid?" I asked.

She nodded enthusiastically. "Absolutely. Harry is a great trainer. He knows his stuff. And a gym is a good investment. But Harry, well, he's never been good with money. He's the live from paycheck-to-paycheck type."

"And you wanted to protect your investment." It made perfect sense. "Why did he get so angry when you said you wouldn't sign? Well, wouldn't sign *yet*," I corrected.

She ran a hand around her neck and crossed to look out the window. "I could see that he was rushing it. To have a successful business, you need a solid foundation. He said he had clients lined up waiting to join, but that will not do you any good if you can't afford your rent or have no equipment. But in Harry's mind, he was ready to go *now*. He didn't see the value in having a business plan. He called it fluffy paperwork."

"I talked to him earlier," I said, watching for her reaction, "and he was pretty aggressive. Is that his usual style?"

She shook her head. "I've noticed that in him recently too. He's agitated and stressed. Him biting my head off yesterday when I said we weren't ready to sign the loan papers yet? That was so out of character for him."

I glanced toward Ben to gauge his thoughts. "Maybe something else is going on?" he suggested. "Other than the gym stuff. Is he in financial trouble?"

"It's possible. Like I said, he lives paycheck to paycheck, with little to no savings. He was furious when I said I wasn't prepared to sign for the loan yet. Said he needed the money now." She looked from Ben to me.

"Mad enough to kill you?"

"No," she said emphatically. "I've known Harry since I was a kid, and believe me, we've had some doozy fights. Yesterday's disagreement was nothing. Plus, if he killed me, he'd never get the money. So, no motive. What's his alibi? Where was he when I was stabbed?"

"He was with a client. I'll follow that up to verify." Pulling out my phone, I clicked on a photo. "Do you remember this guy?"

Gianna peered at the screen, then snorted. "That's Troy Barnes. I represented his wife, Elissa, in their divorce."

"I take it you won?"

"Of course."

"Is that why Troy was so mad at you?"

Gianna waved a hand in dismissal. "The man was drunk, but yes, he was screeching that he'd lost everything, and it was all my fault." She paced back and forth. "This isn't new. The majority of my clients are female, and the majority of my cases I win, so yes, I have a lot of disgruntled ex-husbands gunning for me."

"Enough to kill you?" Ben stepped into her path, and she stopped to look at him.

"No. Absolutely not."

I exchanged a look with Ben. Neither of us believed her. Time to track down Troy Barnes and see what he had to say for himself.

"That man lost his business, home, and family, ended up bankrupt and in rehab, thanks to your dead divorce attorney." Roy Mullins tugged at the lapels of his ill-fitting suit jacket, sweat staining the armpits. The buttons of his white button-down strained under the pressure of the enormous gut hanging over his belt.

"Where is he now?" Roy owned the car dealership I currently stood in. The same car dealership where Troy Barnes worked.

"He hasn't turned up for work today."

I could tell Roy wanted to defend his employee, but the way his eyes darted away from me toward the cars in the lot told me he wasn't one hundred percent sure Troy didn't kill Gianna.

"I take it he was supposed to work today?"

Roy nodded. "Weekends are our busiest period. And since Troy barely sees his kid—thanks to that court order—he volunteered for the weekend shift."

I handed Roy my business card. "If he turns up, have him call me."

"I'll let him know you swung by." Roy saluted, then hurried off to greet the couple who'd just arrived and were peering in the window of a yellow Corvette.

"That was a bust," I muttered, heading back to my car.

"Not necessarily," Ben replied. "We know Troy Barnes had a powerful motive to want Gianna dead."

"But he was rebuilding his life. Why risk it?" I jerked my thumb toward the used car dealership behind us.

Ben snorted. "That's hardly a career choice. Selling beat-up, second-hand vehicles wouldn't bring in much of a paycheck. And the fact he didn't show up for work today? Suspish."

"Suspish? What is that, teen speak?"

"It means suspicious," Ben said defensively, arms crossing over his chest as he slouched in the passenger seat. "And yeah," he cleared his throat, "I may have been watching a little too much Bailey Sarian lately."

"Is that a TV show?"

"YouTube channel."

"How on Earth are you managing to watch YouTube videos?"

Ben grinned, perking up. "Easy. I discovered I can do my *thing* on any computer or device turned on. So many people leave their laptops on or their iPads. I just have to touch it, and I can pretty much do what I want, provided they have the appropriate apps installed."

"It's Seb, isn't it? I bet he's deliberately leaving his computer on so you can use it."

Ben blinked, then cleared his throat. "What makes you think it's Seb?"

Oh, it was Seb. "Because he's is pretty intuitive. He cottoned on quickly that I could talk to ghosts. I think he senses your presence. He knows about your ability to ride the data waves, so he probably figured if he left his computer on for you, you could...what? Have unlimited access to the shopping websites." A horrible thought occurred to me. "Oh my God, you can't order stuff online, can you?"

Ben clasped a hand to his chest as if offended I'd suggest such a thing. "Technically? Yes. Morally? No."

I tossed my phone into the center console. "Here. Do your thing. Use my app and find an address for Troy Barnes. I think he may be our killer."

9

The only address Ben could find for Troy was the house where he'd lived with his ex, Elissa. The one Elissa won in the divorce. I pulled into the driveway and admired the two-story colonial with an attached garage and neatly mowed front lawn.

"Notice that?" I nodded toward a boarded-up window by the front door.

"Uh-huh. You think Troy's responsible?"

"Hard to imagine otherwise."

A voice rang out from the neighbor's yard. "They're not home!" I turned to see a pear-shaped woman with short, pink hair and lime green, wire-framed glasses washing her car in the driveway.

"We're looking for Troy Barnes," I said.

"He's not allowed to come around here." She

sniffed, tossing the sponge into the bucket of sudsy water and pushing her glasses back up her nose.

"Why not?"

"Came by last week, drunk off his ass, and got in a fight with his wife. Broke a window."

"Wow. Makes sense. I'd be salty if I lost this place in a divorce." The house was lovely, but what would smashing a window achieve? Other than breaching a PPO. "Do you have any idea where I can find him?"

"Don't know, don't care. As long as he stays away from this neighborhood, that's all I care about. Man is a menace."

"Is his ex-wife around?"

"Elissa? She's probably off with her boyfriend. Where is anyone's guess, though. Look, I'm sorry, I've gotta go clean up. Troy isn't here." Picking up her bucket, she tossed the contents on the front lawn, retrieved the sponge that had flown out with the water, and headed inside.

"Okay, super sleuth, now what?" Ben asked, resuming his shotgun position in my car. Sliding into the driver's seat, I drummed my thumbs on the steering wheel while I thought for a minute. "We've hit a dead end. No pun intended."

"You know, you could always ask Galloway about Troy's last known address. If the guy violated a PPO," Ben pointed to the broken window, "they'd have his current info on file."

I cricked my neck. Yes, I could definitely do that, but then I'd be tipping the love of my life off on where we were with our investigation, which didn't sit well with my competitive side. "Maybe," I said, pulling away from Elissa Barnes's house and heading home. Time to put my fingers to the keyboard and do some digging. If all else fails, I'll send Ben to the police station to dig around in their database.

"I know you and Kade have this little wager going on," Ben said beside me. I could feel a lecture coming on. With a herculean effort, I controlled my eyeballs and forbid them from rolling. Instead, I focused on the road ahead and half-listened to Ben.

"If you worked together, you'd solve the case quicker. And then you could concentrate on the wedding."

The last part caught my attention.

I almost ran off the road. "Wedding planning? Are you worried that I'm not spending enough time planning *my* wedding? Relax, dude, it's months away." One thing about my macho, manly man best friend. He had a distinctly feminine side. His obsession with the shopping channel, for one. And my wedding coming a close second. Maybe it was because Ben never married before he passed and was now living vicariously through me. Or perhaps he simply liked big poofy meringue-type dresses. Who knows? But ever since Galloway asked me to marry him, Ben had been a tad obsessive about the wedding. Just like everyone else in my family.

"I'm not worried."

Casting him a look from the corner of my eye, it was clear he was definitely worried. The crease between his brows gave it away. And the way the corners of his mouth turned down. Either annoyed or sulking, I wasn't sure which.

"Oh, good. I'd hate to see your worried face, anyway, back to the case. Yes, I could go to Galloway for help, but I'm not at that point yet. Give me some credit. I'm actually pretty good at this whole PI thing. Why don't you visit Gianna for a while? She said she wanted to stay at her office, that *working* with her files gave her comfort."

"Good idea. Maybe I can shake something loose from her memory. She had to have seen her killer. She was stabbed from the front. No way she could have missed it."

"Truth."

But he'd gone. I was talking to an empty seat.

"Mom! Mom! Mom!" I could hear Bandit before I saw her, her paws scratching on the floorboards as she hurtled herself through the house. I'd forgotten I'd had to give her a fur cut, so when she appeared, I was momentarily taken aback at the sight of her. I had not done this raccoon justice.

"Zoinks."

I surveyed the damage. One patch of fur in the middle of her back had escaped unscathed. The rest of her was a ragged mess. "How would you feel about a trip to the groomer?" I asked, scratching the top of her head when she stood on her hind legs, ready for some loving.

"Not the vet?"

"Not the vet," I agreed. "I'll find a cat groomer who can help. Thor can come too."

Speak of the devil—Thor waddled down the hallway, stomach bulging. The diet wasn't working. I wondered if I got a treadmill if I could convince him to use it?

"Thor can do what?" Thor asked, rubbing his face against my shin with a purr. He really was the cutest cat, round face like a teddy bear. Even if he was a chonkers, he was still cute. Sadly, I couldn't say the same for his attitude.

"Come to the groomer. Bandit's fur needs fixing. And it wouldn't hurt for you to have a groom." In for a penny, in for a pound.

"What's a groom?" Bandit asked.

"Someone brushing your fur," I explained.

"Oh! Like my spa yesterday?" She clapped her little paws together in delight.

"Yes! Only better."

"You're not putting me in the sink and turning on the faucet." Thor turned and walked away, tail flicking with what I assumed was irritation at the mention of the 'spa.'

"Yeah, well," I called after him, "if you hadn't encouraged her to break into the pantry, none of this would have happened!"

"Wasn't me!" he shouted back.

"Liar!"

"Are you angry, Mom?" Bandit sat at my feet, crestfallen.

Shaking my head, I scooped her up into my arms and cuddled her to my chest. "No, sweetheart. Not angry. Just disappointed." Son of a gun, I was officially my mother.

Dropping a kiss on Bandit's head, I set her on the floor and pulled out my phone, searching for cat groomers who were open on a Sunday. Eventually, I found one who agreed to take on a raccoon, and they had an opening. Bundling Bandit and Thor into their respective pet carriers and loading them into the car was a workout in itself. Thor let his displeasure be known the entire drive, convincing Bandit that we were, indeed, going to the vet because every time Thor had been in his carrier, that's where he'd ended up and that one time he'd come home without a particular part of his anatomy, and he had *not* forgotten.

Pulling up outside the front of the groomer's shop, I lifted Thor out first.

"There!" I declared. "Does that look like the vet?"

His orange eyes peered through the grate of his carrier. "You're taking us to a shelter?" he wailed and began turning in circles in his carrier, which was quite a feat since he filled the entire thing. But the jerky movements made the carrier challenging to hold. I released the handle and wrapped my arms around it, clutching it to my chest in an awkward embrace in case I dropped him.

"Sshhh," I soothed, realizing I'd messed up. "The groomer works out of the animal shelter. Look, you can see the sign, just over there." I pointed to a cute little sign that simply said '*groomer*' in a fancy font. "I'm not giving you up. I'd never give you up. I love you. And Bandit. We're just here to give your fur a good brush and make you smell nice." I didn't mention the bath that went along with the brush.

"What's wrong with the way I smell?"

I rolled my eyes. "Nothing. Honestly, Thor, I brought you along to help keep Bandit calm. You don't really need a groom, but she does. Badly. Can you help me out?" I belatedly realized I should have led with this tactic from the get-go, for Thor immediately calmed down, his shrewd eyes going from me to the animal shelter to Bandit. "You're not leaving her here, are you?"

"Absolutely not."

"Okay." And just like that, all was calm. I took Thor in first and checked in with the shelter receptionist, who led me through to the groomer, who had their own small waiting room. I left Thor and retrieved Bandit.

"Where's Thor?" she whispered, lying flat in the bottom of her carrier. I felt like a monster.

"He's okay. He's waiting for us inside," I assured her. "He got a little scared, but he's fine now."

"I'm not scared."

I chuckled at her lie but played along. "I know you're not because you're a very brave raccoon."

"But Thor was scared." She blinked and gave a slight nod of her head.

"He was. But you know Thor," I warned her. "He won't admit it."

"Okay."

I chewed my lip, running through options in my head. Initially, I was going to have Thor go first to show Bandit there was nothing to be afraid of. Now I wondered if it should be the other way around.

"How do you feel about going first?" I asked Bandit, carrying her inside. "I think Thor is a little nervous."

Bandit nodded, almost back to her usual self. "Yes! I can go first and show Thor I'm brave."

After depositing Bandit's carrier on a chair next to Thor's, I headed to the counter.

"Audrey, is it?" The woman dressed in a colorful pet-themed smock had a voice like rusty nails, and judging by the deep lines around her mouth, I assumed it was from smoking. Her skin was deeply tanned and resembled leather.

"Yes. I'm here with Thor, a British shorthair, and Bandit, a raccoon."

"We don't often groom raccoons," she said, glancing over at Bandit, who was peering through the bars of her carrier at us. Thor was as far back in his carrier as he could get, and my heart hurt for him. I'd misjudged how traumatic the whole experience would be, and now I wished I'd left him at home.

"I never thought I'd have to bring her to a groomer," I confessed. "But she got into some peanut butter last night, and I couldn't get it out, so I cut it out. I realized today what a woeful job I did, so I'm hoping the groomer can help?"

"How bad is the cut?"

"It's bad." I leaned closer and dropped my voice. "You may need to shave her."

The woman, Shirley, her nametag said, snorted. "I'll let Michelle know. Shaving would be the last resort, but she may be able to do something trendy with the cut. You up for that?"

"Anything would be an improvement."

Shirley passed me a card and pen. "Hand over the

raccoon, and I'll take her back while you fill out their details."

"Her name is Bandit." I hurried to pick up Bandit's carrier, squatting in front of it to wiggle my fingers through the grate and rub her nose. "It's all going to be okay," I whispered. "You're going to look amazing. And it won't hurt, not a bit, I promise." I silently prayed that the groomer wouldn't nick her with anything sharp and make a liar out of me.

"I'm brave, Mom!" Bandit declared with such conviction that my heart constricted on a wave of love. Was this what it was like having kids? When you had to hand them over to someone else and constantly worried that they'd be okay without you? Gah, I wasn't sure I could take it. It was hard enough with my pets, let alone a tiny human, further cementing my stance on not having children.

I sat and waited, Thor trembling in his carrier beside me. I kept one arm draped over it, my fingers poking through the side so I could touch him and reassure him he was not about to die, all the while feeling like the worst pet parent in the world. I should have asked Ben about this, but I'd assumed he'd taken Thor to the groomer at least once in his lifetime. Apparently not.

Eventually, Bandit was returned, and it was Thor's turn. He'd relaxed somewhat upon seeing Bandit was unscathed and apparently happy.

"Mom!" she declared upon seeing me. "The nice lady used this funny thing that buzzed and vibrated on my skin, and then she took my fur away!"

"I take it she's shaved?" I asked Shirley, who grinned and nodded.

"Couldn't save much. You really hacked into it. What did you use, garden shears?"

I jerked, taken aback. I knew it was bad, but garden shears? Come on, I'm not a Neanderthal. I used kitchen scissors thank you very much.

"Anyway, Michelle did a cute little design on her back. Hope you like it," Shirley said, accepting Thor's carrier and turning away.

The next hour was spent listening to Thor's yowling. He let his displeasure be known every step of the way. Honestly, I was hard-pressed not to laugh because of his outraged cries of, "*Don't touch me there!*" to "*What do you think you're doing with that*?" to a more subdued, "*Actually, that's not so bad, do that again.*"

Shirley reappeared. "Michelle's just finishing up with Mr. Vocal back there." She jerked her thumb behind her. "If it's okay with you, we'll settle up now?"

"Sure. And I'll put Bandit in the car, so we can get out of your hair when Thor comes out."

Shirley rang us up, and my eyes watered at the bill. Bandit had better not need another groom in her entire life, or I'd have to send her out to get a job. It was not cheap. But I paid and added a tip, then took her out to the car, securing her carrier on the back seat with the seatbelt looped through the handle, then went back inside.

Thor's carrier was sitting on the counter, with Shirley resting her elbows on the counter next to it, waiting.

"Thank you. And Michelle," I said. "I really do appreciate you fitting me in today. And I'm sorry he was so noisy. I had no idea."

Shirley smiled. "It's what we do."

"Is Michelle here? I'd like to thank her personally." And give her a tip. Despite already forking out an obscene amount of money for her services, I still felt the poor woman deserved extra for what Thor had put her through. It can't be easy grooming an animal that cries the entire time, and since she couldn't understand what he was saying, she'd be at a loss to know what the problem was.

"She's gone," Shirley said.

"Gone?" But how? It had been all of five minutes since she was done with Thor.

"She's stressed, in part because she has such huge shoes to fill."

"She does?"

"Yeah, she's new here. Our other groomer quit, and of course, all of our clientele loved Susan, so yeah, Michelle feels like she's not measuring up. Grooming is a very personal thing... and when you find a groomer who does a great job, not just the cut but not stressing the animal too much and reporting back something they've noticed, it's hard to lose them.

"Michelle has been dealing with people who expect her to have the same multi-tasking skills as Susan, and she's simply not there yet. So, she's been shouted at, snarked at, sniped at."

I blinked, not knowing what to say. I hadn't done any of those things, and as a first-time customer, I had no expectations other than having a groomed pet at the end of it. "Well, tell her from me next time you see her that she did a great job. I appreciate it."

"She's got man troubles," Shirley confided, keen to gossip about her coworker.

"That sucks." Poor Michelle. Stressed at work, trouble at home.

"Got herself mixed up with a divorced fella who really needs to get his life sorted before he jumps into another relationship, but Michelle? She thinks with her heart, which really only leads to one thing. Heartache."

My ears pricked up. "Do you know who the guy is?" I mean, there were a ton of divorced guys in Firefly Bay. What were the chances my new groomer was involved with my suspect?

Turns out one hundred percent.

"Some loser called Troy Barnes. You know him?"

"Actually, I'm trying to track him down," I said,

leaning my elbows on the counter and leaning in, matching Shirley's pose. "I don't suppose you know where I could find him?"

Shirley thought for a minute, fingers drumming on the counter. "Usually, he's at Michelle's place, but I know they're fighting cos he didn't come home last night, and you and I both know what that means... he was out carousing with other women."

Or killing them.

"Where does Michelle live?"

"Out on Henderson Road, just past the red barn."

"Cool, I'll swing by. Well, thanks for everything. You—and Michelle—have been a great help." *Lady, you have no idea.*

"Anytime. Have a nice day." Shirley nodded and continued to lean on the counter, watching as I picked up Thor and carried him out to the car. I couldn't believe my luck. My side quest dealing with Bandit's fur situation had resulted in a solid lead on my suspect's whereabouts. All I had to do was drop my fur babies at home, then Troy Barnes was in my sights.

10

*B*en hadn't returned from Gianna's by the time I dropped Bandit and Thor at home. Thor had scampered straight upstairs to sleep off the trauma of being groomed while Bandit happily trotted after him, suffering no ill effects. Most of her body was shaved, except her paws, head, tail, and the patch on her back. Michelle had shaved around it, creating a cute paw print. Adorable. I made a mental note to thank Michelle personally when I caught up with her. Which was hopefully now.

Jumping back into my Honda CR-V, I headed out to Henderson Road, belatedly realizing I should have spent a little time looking up Michelle's actual address, for all I had to go on was a red barn. Turns out I needn't have worried, for as I approached the only red barn I could see on Henderson Road, I spotted a trailer parked next to it with a faded red pickup and a gray sedan out front.

"Bingo." Standing in the trailer's doorway was a woman wearing pet-themed scrubs like Shirley's. This had to be Michelle. And she was cheesed off, tossing armfuls of clothing out the door to flutter all over the ground.

"Babe, c'mon!" The man standing outside watching the carnage shook his head and began scooping up the clothes, tossing them into the cab of his pickup.

I pulled up next to the sedan, drawing Michelle's attention. She was pretty, in a tired, worn down kinda way. Her blonde hair was from a bottle, the strands dull, the two inches of dark roots giving her away. And her face was gaunt as if she hadn't eaten a decent meal in...forever.

"Who is she?" Michelle screeched, not at me, but at who had to be Troy Barnes, for now that I was closer, I could see the scar above one eye. His hair was collar length and needed washing and brushing, his jaw covered in a thick stubble. His worn jeans, scuffed boots, and faded T-shirt matched his persona—weary, just like Michelle. Maybe that's why they'd been drawn to each other, two kindred souls, down on their luck.

"How the hell should I know?" Troy shouted back, snatching up a book she'd thrown at him, narrowly missing his head.

"Is she who you were with last night?" Tears

streamed down Michelle's face, taking her mascara with them, leaving black smudges under her eyes. "It's her, isn't it?" The screaming got worse, and I realized I'd walked smack dab into the middle of a domestic.

"Listen, lady, I don't know who you are or what you want, but now is not a good time," Troy said to me, picking up his belongings and tossing them in his truck.

"Troy Barnes?"

He paused, eyes narrowing. "Who wants to know?"

"Audrey Fitzgerald, private investigator." I held out a business card which he ignored.

"Like I said, now's not a good time."

The trailer door slammed, and we both looked at it. Seemed Michelle had evicted Troy, and now all his worldly possessions, such as they were, were lying on the ground. I began helping him pick them up and deposit them in the pickup, feeling kinda sorry for the guy. He really was down on his luck. Was it enough to make him a killer?

"Where were you last night, say between six and nine?"

"Why do you want to know?"

"Gianna Tate was killed last night."

He froze for a second before straightening and shoving his hands into the front pockets of his jeans. "I didn't kill her, okay?"

"No? But you wanted to. Witnesses overheard you in The Bay threatening to kill her."

"I went there to get my life back," Troy said, shifting his weight from one foot to the other. "Do you know what it's like to lose everything? To lose the respect of your friends? Family?"

"Not really. Care to tell me?"

"I went to rehab. Anger management. When I got back, I had to work three jobs to pay back the lawyers. I was finally getting on top of things. Stopped into The Bay, and I saw that blonde's shiny hair, those flashy rings, the designer threads."

"And you saw red?"

He nodded, bowing his head. "I hadn't had a drink in months, and the one time I do, and *she's* there. So, I had a drink to settle my nerves. Then I got drunk. Words were exchanged, and if you want the honest to God truth, I don't remember much of what was said."

"Then what happened? You follow her home?"

"I passed out in my truck."

"Some alibi, Troy. Anyone able to verify that?"

He snorted. "Of course not." Finished collecting his possessions, he gave me a mock salute, climbed into his truck, and gunned the engine, dirt flying as he peeled out of the driveway. I followed suit, minus the dirt flinging, deciding now was not the best time to thank Michelle for her grooming skills. I somehow thought she wouldn't be appreciative of my praise.

"Is she here?" Seb asked, perched on a barstool in my kitchen, a glass of red wine in his hand.

I shook my head. "No. I think she's at her happy place—her office—that woman loves to work."

I poured a glass of wine for myself and clinked my glass with Seb's. "Cheers."

"Come on then, tell me all about it. Who are your suspects?"

I grinned at his enthusiasm, planting myself on a stool next to him. He reminded me of me, which was probably why I liked him so much.

"So, we have her personal trainer and childhood friend, Harry Watts. Apparently, Gianna was going to co-sign a loan so Harry can open his own gym."

"Was? She changed her mind?"

I shrugged. "Not changed her mind. More delayed the signing. She said he was rushing things, didn't have a proper business plan, and was just pulling numbers out of thin air."

"I guess as an attorney, she'd know." Seb took another sip of wine, swirling the red liquid in his glass. The day had flown by, and now the sun was dipping on the horizon, sending shards of orange and purple across the sky.

"Yep. And she specializes not only in family law but also business law. So yeah, she'd know, alright. It surprises me that Harry would think she wouldn't notice him taking shortcuts."

"Why the rush?"

It was my turn to shrug. "Excitement, I guess? I don't know. I need to dig a little further into Harry. He said they grew up together, and she confirmed it. Is he the one behind the blackmail threat? Did he get mad that she delayed signing the loan papers, so he decided to extort money out of her instead?"

Seb did a double-take. "Back up the truck!" He waggled a finger at me. "Blackmail threat?"

"Oh yeah, didn't I mention that? Gianna was about to hire me to find out who was attempting to blackmail her. She received an email saying they had risqué photos from her youth."

"How much did they want?"

"One hundred thousand."

Seb whistled. "Ballsy."

I sighed. "I just don't think our blackmailer is our killer. It doesn't make sense. There was only one email with the demand for money but no instruction on how that money was to be delivered or a deadline. Which tells me to expect a second email sometime soon. If the blackmailer wanted cold hard cash, it wouldn't be in their best interest to then murder the person they were trying to extort."

"Hmmm. Agreed. Let's park that. We'll circle back to it."

"Okay, Sherlock," I teased. "Next up is Troy Barnes. Gianna represented his wife in their divorce last year."

"I take it she won?"

"Of course. Completely destroyed Troy. He went bankrupt."

"Oooh, motive!"

"Exactly. *And* he was seen arguing with her Saturday afternoon at The Bay."

"Oh, he's our man. For sure."

"That could well be, but first, we need evidence. Just because he has motive and opportunity doesn't mean he actually did it."

"Listen to you, all Nancy Drew." Seb nudged me, and I wobbled, spilling my wine.

Tsking under his breath, Seb grabbed some paper towels and cleaned up. "Hope you're not serving red wine at your wedding, girl."

I guffawed. "I haven't even thought about it."

Seb looked at me, eyes perfectly round orbs in his handsome face, popping a hip. He really was pin-up model type handsome. How he was single was beyond me. He'd make an incredible catch for some lucky guy.

Dropping his voice low, he said, "Tell me you've started planning."

I lifted one shoulder and brought my glass to my lips, taking another sip of wine.

Dialing his campiness up to one thousand, Seb planted a hand on his chest and declared, "Audrey

Fitzgerald, do I need to stage an intervention? Where are you at?" He began ticking off on his fingers. "Booked a venue? Dress? Hair and makeup? Cake?"

"None of the above," I admitted. "We've only just set the date."

"Church or ..."

"Or," I stated vehemently. "Galloway is in agreement on that. We won't be getting married in a church."

"That's wonderful news, girlfriend." Seb fluttered his impossibly thick and dark lashes at me. "Because you are looking at a bona fide officiant! I'd be honored to officiate at your wedding."

My jaw dropped. "Really? I didn't know you were an officiant! That would be amazing." I could already see Amanda having an absolute conniption.

"Oh, I've been one for oodles." Seb finished cleaning up my spilled wine and resumed his seat. "Mostly same-sex marriages, but I'll make an exception for you."

"I'm blessed."

"Dad! Dad! Dad!" Bandit came barreling downstairs and heading for the front door. Thor followed at a more sedate pace.

"What's up with them?" Seb asked.

"Galloway's home." I smiled, sliding off my stool and going to greet him.

I found him in the entryway, ambushed by two

furry critters. He was cooing over Bandit's trendy haircut, and she was basking in the attention. I waited, sipping my wine and swooning over how lucky I was to have a man like Kade Galloway in my life. Patient. Strong. Sexy. Funny. Did I mention patient?

"Hey, babe." Finished with the animals, he crossed to me in two long strides, wrapped an arm around my waist, and tugged me against him, kissing me long and hard. My heart stuttered in my chest and then took off at a wild gallop.

"Mmmm." he lifted his head slightly, his breath hot on my mouth. "You taste nice."

I held up my glass. "That'd be the wine. Want one?"

He dropped another quick kiss on my lips and squeezed my rear. "Of course." Following me into the kitchen, he greeted Seb. "Hey, how's it going?"

"Fantastic. We were just talking about your wedding." Seb reminded me of a golden retriever, full of excitement, tail wagging.

"Oh?" Galloway arched a brow.

"Seb's an officiant, and he's offered to marry us," I said, grabbing a wine glass from the overhead cabinet and pouring Galloway a hefty serving.

"Audrey told you we're not getting married in a church then?"

Seb nodded. "She did. Which is why I offered. I take it that's all you've organized? Nothing booked?" You couldn't miss the slightly horrified tone in his voice, and Galloway looked at me, a sexy smirk curling his lips. My heart rate shot up again. I'd need an appointment with a cardiologist if this kept up.

"There's plenty of time," Galloway said, echoing my own sentiments exactly.

"Clearly, you have never been married before," Seb declared. "Not that that's a bad thing. But weddings? They take time to organize, and stuff needs to be booked in advance. Waaaay in advance."

My brows lowered. "He's throwing words around like venue, cake, dress, hair, and makeup." I pouted, snuggling into Galloway's chest.

"How dare he." Galloway chuckled, rubbing a soothing hand up and down my back. "Why don't you hire him to be your wedding planner? Then you won't have to worry about it."

Seb and I gasped in unison. Pushing out of Galloway's arms, I looked at Seb, grinning so wide that his white teeth practically blinded me.

"You're hired!" I declared.

"Done!" he agreed.

Amanda was going to kill me.

11

"*How* goes your investigation?" Galloway asked once we'd done clinking glasses to seal the deal.

I blew out a breath. "It would help if Gianna could actually remember her murder."

"That's cheating." Galloway winked. "Hit a dead end, have we?"

I snorted at his pun. "You're only asking cos you've hit a dead end." I was bluffing. Galloway had an excellent poker face, among other things, so I wasn't really sure if he'd unearthed a viable suspect or not.

"Wanna scrap the wager and pool resources?" he offered, watching me over the top of his glass as he took a mouthful, then, as the flavors hit his tongue, pulling the glass away and staring at it. "This is really nice."

"Thanks," Seb said. "This little cabernet sauvignon is from my collection. But sadly, I've already told Audrey she can't have red wine at the wedding. She'll only spill it on her dress."

I held up a hand in a stop gesture. "No more talk of the wedding. Honestly, I've had Mom and Amanda on my back today about my dress—sidenote guys, I'm not getting married in white—and I'm just about done talking about it."

"I don't care what you wear. Turn up in jeans and a tank for all I care. Just turn up," Galloway said, curling his fingers around mine and giving my hand a comforting squeeze.

"Awwwww." Seb swooned by my side. "You guys are the cutest. And of course, you're not wearing white. Not with your coloring. Honestly, some people have no clue."

"Back to Gianna's murder. So, you're admitting defeat?" I narrowed my eyes at Galloway, who grinned at me, totally disarming my thought processes.

"Are you?" he shot back.

"Pft. Of course not. I'm still investigating."

"As are we."

"Oh, stop it." Seb flapped a hand at us. "You know you work better together. You're both too proud—and competitive—to admit it."

"He's right," we said in unison and then laughed.

"Okay, I'll go first." Galloway sobered and took

another mouthful of wine before holding up one finger. "Suspect one. Harry Watts."

I nodded. "Yep. He's on my list. Gianna was going to co-sign a loan for a new gym, but she's holding back as she thought he was half-assing the business plan."

"I knew about the loan but didn't know why the delay." Galloway inclined his head. "That's good to know."

"Does he have an alibi? He told me he was with a client."

"He does have an alibi, but he wasn't with a client. He was at a building on East Street where he's just signed the lease for his new gym."

"What? Where did he get the money for the lease? Gianna hasn't signed the loan papers yet."

"Excellent question. But we have CCTV footage of him outside the building at the time of her murder."

That ruled out Harry Watts as Gianna's killer. She'd be pleased to hear that. It would be awful to know someone you considered a friend had murdered you.

"I spoke with Troy Barnes this afternoon," I said. "He got in an argument with Gianna yesterday afternoon at The Bay. Turns out Gianna represented his wife in their divorce and totally annihilated the man. He had an ax to grind for sure. And he threatened to kill her."

Galloway's ears perked up. "Does he have an alibi?"

"Not a good one. He said he got drunk and passed out in his truck."

"Do you know where the truck was parked? We may be able to get traffic cam footage."

"Errr, sorry, I didn't think to ask." Darn it, if Ben had been with me, he'd have probably prompted me to ask exactly that, but I'd made a rookie mistake.

"No problem. Troy is on our list of suspects too, and we're pulling him in for questioning. We'll get the info from him then."

"I'm not sure where he's actually living. I found him at Michelle's trailer out on Henderson Road, and she was throwing him out. I don't know if he was living with her or if he just occasionally spent the night."

"Michelle?"

"She's the groomer behind Bandit's new look. She works out at the shelter—they have a separate grooming business on-site—and her coworker, Shirley, likes to gossip. She filled me in that Michelle was having man trouble."

"And that led you to Troy? Impressive."

"It was a long shot that paid off." I blew off his praise but inside, I was glowing.

"Sounds to me like case closed," Seb said. "Troy's your man."

"Maybe," Galloway said. "But we need the evidence to back that up. He's definitely got motive, but did he have opportunity? If he was drunk, how did he manage to get into Gianna's home without anyone noticing?"

"Maybe he wasn't drunk," Seb offered. "Maybe it was all an act, to give himself an alibi. No one is going to think the drunk guy did it."

"Or maybe he'd already slept it off. She was killed early evening. The altercation at The Bay was early afternoon. A quick nap in his truck and then off to commit a bit of murder. Shirley told me Michelle was upset because Troy hadn't come home the night before. Did he spend all night in his truck? From early evening until dawn? That doesn't seem likely."

"The timeline is off," Galloway agreed.

"You have a point about the killer getting into Gianna's house without being seen." I mulled over all we knew. "If it was Harry or Troy, they'd have had to be pretty stealthy."

"You said it was a pre-party party, right?" Seb asked.

I nodded. "Correct."

"I don't know about you, but the parties I've been to tend to be on the loud side. If everyone is having a good time, I think it's relatively easy to sneak in and out again without being noticed."

"The ballroom was off to the side of the foyer," I conceded.

"With music blaring and a disco ball flashing," Galloway added.

"So, the killer... what? Managed to get inside and

then hide out in Gianna's bedroom? They couldn't have known her necklace would break and that she would go upstairs."

"Is that what happened?" Galloway asked, and I realized I hadn't told him what Gianna *could* remember. I quickly rectified that, telling him about her broken necklace and how she took it upstairs to her dressing room to put it in the jewelry box.

"She doesn't remember seeing anyone upstairs. Nor being killed."

Galloway was absently swirling the wine in his glass, lost in thought. "What if this wasn't premeditated?" he said. "What if Gianna surprised the killer, and they reacted instinctively, stabbing her so they could get away."

"Surprised them? Doing what?" Then it hit me. "Someone was breaking in! Under cover of the party. Sneak in, steal her... what? Jewelry? She mentioned she has a jewelry box in her dressing room, and judging by the rings, bracelets, and watches she wears, I'd say they were worth a small fortune." I dragged in a breath. "So, the thief is upstairs, raiding her jewelry box when Gianna unexpectedly turns up!"

"And," Seb jumped in, "you probably have tools of the trade with you when you're stealing jewelry. Something to jimmy a lock if need be?"

"Like a screwdriver," Galloway said. "She was stabbed with something round."

"Find the screwdriver, find the killer. Troy Barnes drove a pick-up. What's the bet he had a toolbox in the back?"

"Hey, the gangs all here." Ben suddenly appeared, making me jump.

Seb grabbed my arm, fingers curling into my flesh hard enough to leave a mark. His eyes darted around the room. "The atmosphere just changed," he stage whispered. "Someone's here, aren't they?"

"Ben's here," I said. "I swear you must be psychic or clairvoyant or something."

"There's a... I don't know what, a change in the air? I kinda feel it when he's around," Seb explained.

"I get the change in the air," I said. "Whenever Ben touches me, I get a cold shiver. Maybe you're feeling that."

"Fascinating," Ben drawled, settling himself onto the stool next to Seb. "So, what are we all doing?"

"We're discussing Gianna's murder," I told him.

"I thought you two were in competition," Ben pointed from me to Galloway and back again.

I shrugged. "We were. Now we're pooling resources."

"Cos I told them they work better together," Seb chimed in, despite only hearing my side of the conversation. "Oh, also, I'm going to be the celebrant at their wedding. And Audrey's wedding planner!" Something told me Seb desperately wanted to clap his hands together in glee but was reining in his excitement, probably for Galloway's benefit.

Ben raised a brow, much like Galloway does, and I felt a warm fluttering in my heart. My two best men were so similar yet very different, and I loved them both dearly. Gah, I was getting sappy in my old age.

"Yeah, well, I need someone to keep Mom and Amanda out of my hair. Seb volunteered," I said in the way of defense. "But—again—no more talk of the wedding tonight, please. We were brainstorming and coming up with a theory."

"On?" Ben asked.

"Gianna's killer. We think someone snuck into her house, using the party as a cover, with the intent to steal her jewelry. Only Gianna unexpectedly returned to her bedroom and caught them in the act."

Ben thought over what I'd said, slowly nodding. "Sounds feasible."

"So, we just need Gianna to look at her jewelry collection and tell us if anything is missing."

"Easy enough to do. She's at home now."

Tossing back the rest of my wine, I slammed my glass onto the counter, snapping the stem. "Shoot."

"Lucky you'd finished that," Seb said. "It would be sacrilegious to waste this wine."

"Did you cut yourself?" Galloway reached for me, his fingers wrapping around my wrist to examine my hand. I wanted to shoo away his concern, but I enjoyed his touch too much.

"I'm fine. Come on, drink up. We need to get over to Gianna's house."

"What's the rush?"

"She's there now. I don't know how long she'll stay since her happy place appears to be her office."

Seb slid off his stool and picked up the bottle of wine. "You guys go do whatcha gotta do. I'm going to take this home with me."

"Thanks for dropping by, Seb. And for everything else." I reached up and kissed his cheek.

"Anytime, darl, I'm off to research all things wedding."

I chewed my lip, watching him practically bounce out the back door, heading toward the gate between our properties.

"I'm worried I've unleashed a monster," I whispered, turning to Galloway, who was finishing his wine—sans smashing the glass.

"Remember, you have the power to veto any ideas he comes up with," he said. "Don't worry, it'll be fine. All that matters is you and me. The rest of it is fluff."

"If you two are going to continue making googly eyes at each other, I'm not riding with you. I'll meet you at Gianna's," Ben teased, pretending our affection was making him puke.

"Go ahead." I waved him away. "We'll see you there."

"Ben?" Galloway asked, tugging me close.

"Ben," I agreed, melting against him. "He's gone. We're alone."

"Perfect."

12

*T*wilight bathed Gianna's house in rays of orange, the setting sun casting long shadows on the lawn and reflecting off the windows. Last night, the house had been lit up like a Christmas tree, but now it was dark, silent. Eerily so. Especially when I could hear the faint hum of voices in the distance. Voices no one else could hear.

"What's up?" Galloway noticed my shiver and slung an arm around my shoulders. Wrapping my arm around his waist, I walked side by side with him to the front door. Crime scene tape stretched across the entrance.

"Nothing. Just a ghost thing." I stood to the side, waiting while he lifted the tape and unlocked the door. The voices got louder. Stepping over the threshold, I glanced into the ballroom. It was how it had been left the night before, glasses unwashed on coffee tables, streamers dangling from the curtain rails, balloons deflating on their golden ribbons.

Galloway entwined his fingers through mine and led me upstairs to Gianna's bedroom. It was dark inside the house. The sun had dipped behind the horizon in the few minutes since we first arrived, taking the light. Galloway flicked on the bedroom light, and a crystal chandelier sparkled into life.

The arched opening into the dressing room loomed. Despite hearing Ben and Gianna's voices coming from within the room, I was hesitant to approach. Another shiver danced over my skin, goosebumps following in its path.

"Hey." Galloway turned, cupping my face in his palms, concern flashing in his eyes. "What's wrong?"

"I don't know," I whispered, a deep unease settling in the pit of my stomach. "This place? It's giving me the creeps."

He lowered his voice. "Ghosts? Is someone else here? Someone other than Gianna?"

Maybe that was it. Maybe the house was haunted, and I was picking up on spirits long since passed. It reminded me of the nineteen-twenties gangster ghosts who'd chased me all over town with their spooky black smoke and intimidating presence—and I have to say, not a fan.

Knowing I couldn't stand rooted to the spot in

Gianna's bedroom forever, I let Galloway lead me across the plush carpet to the dressing room, waiting while he flicked on the light, chasing away the shadows.

"Finally!" Ben tapped his watch. "Took you long enough."

I felt a wave of heat wash over my face and shot a look at Galloway. His hair was still mussed where I'd run my fingers through it.

"Urgh, don't tell me. I don't want to know." Ben laughed, looking from me to Galloway and back again.

Gianna looked us up and down and smiled. "Leave them alone. Let them steal a little afternoon delight. Goodness knows we won't get the chance again."

If anything, my cheeks burned even more, and the scabs on my forehead started to itch.

"Audrey?" Galloway was really concerned now.

"It's fine. These two are just teasing me because of... you know." The delay in leaving my house. So we'd stolen a bit of alone time, so what? This was the trouble with ghosts. You never knew when they'd pop up, so with Ben gone and the house to ourselves... well, let's just say we took advantage.

Galloway's head tipped back, and a knowing smile slid across his face. "That we made love?" he teased.

"Let's focus on what we're here for, shall we?" I tried to arch a brow, but both shot up, as usual. Despite plenty of practice, I'd yet to master the one eyebrow arch. Walking around the island bench in Gianna's enormous dressing room, I opened the top drawer. "Is this where your jewelry is kept?"

"Only the costume stuff." Gianna joined me, peering into the drawer. "The real stuff is kept in my safe."

"You have a safe?"

"She has a safe?" Galloway asked. "We didn't find one."

"That's because it's hidden," Gianna said. She pointed to a row of gowns. "Behind those."

I crossed to the floor-length gowns, sorely tempted to stop and take the time to admire them. There was a black one that sparkled, a red one that sparkled, a midnight blue velvet number that felt divine to the touch, and so many more. "It's behind these gowns," I told Galloway. Snapping on a pair of gloves, he pushed the gowns to one side, revealing a framed portrait of Gianna hanging on the wall.

"Oh!" I gasped, hand fluttering to my neck.

Galloway snorted. "Well, that was unexpected."

I turned to Gianna. "You could have warned us."

She smirked. "Surely you're not a prude, Audrey? It's just a nude."

The portrait was of Gianna, reclining on a white blanket on a chaise lounge in front of a fire, without a stitch of clothing. The fact that she was naked aside, the painting was exceptionally well done.

Ben, who'd been standing back, shoved me aside with an icy blast to the ribs so he could get a look. He whistled. "Nice!" He grinned at Gianna, who batted her eyelashes at him.

"Right?" she all but purred.

Gross. Just gross.

"Why hide it back here?" I asked, breaking up their flirtation.

"Because I entertain a lot, and this isn't for guests to view. It's for me. So, I keep it here, away from prying eyes."

"Ask her if the safe is behind the portrait," Galloway said, running his fingers around the frame.

"Yes, it is. There's a catch halfway down on the left. Just press it."

I repeated the instructions to Galloway, who promptly found the switch. The portrait swung out like a door, revealing the safe behind it.

"What's the combination?"

I relayed the information to Galloway, who spun the dial on the safe. Each number clicked into place until the door swung open. Inside was a bundle of papers, a wad of cash, and several jeweler's boxes.

Galloway snapped a photo with his phone. "Ask her if it looks like anything is missing. Has it been disturbed?"

Gianna moved in behind Galloway and peered

over his shoulder. "Nope," she said. "That looks about right."

"She says no." I turned to Gianna, a thought crossing my mind. "You don't think this nude portrait is somehow connected to the blackmail attempt, do you?"

She looked at me in surprise. "You know, I'd never thought of that. This was done some twenty years ago."

"Did you sit live for the artist? Or did they take photographs and work from those?" Because that would explain *a lot*. If an artist had nude photos of Gianna, maybe they'd gotten into the wrong hands. Or even the artist themselves was dabbling in a little bit of blackmail. Maybe they were hard on their luck and needed a boost.

"No photography for exactly the reasons you're thinking." Gianna dashed my theory to pieces. "This portrait took three sittings, and it was just me and Edwardo in his studio in Paris, France."

"Who else knows about the portrait?"

"My housekeeper has probably seen it when putting the gowns away when they come back from the cleaners. Or any staff member who took it upon themselves to snoop amongst my gowns."

"What are you thinking?" Galloway asked, removing the jewelry boxes from the safe and placing them on the island bench.

"That Gianna's murder has priority over the

blackmail attempt, but this can't be a coincidence. Gianna has a *nude* portrait. It wouldn't be a stretch for someone to take a photo of it."

"Any leads on that?" He began opening the jewelry boxes, six in total. I gasped at the twinkle of diamonds in the overhead light. One box alone held six diamond rings. Another had a necklace with a heart-shaped ruby and three diamonds embedded on either side.

"Wow." I whistled. "No wonder these were in the safe. They must be worth millions."

Gianna nodded. "My lawyer has all the documentation as to their value."

"Any missing?" Galloway asked, and Gianna shook her head.

"She says no."

Galloway snapped photos and then began putting everything back in the safe. "Audrey? The blackmail case?" he reminded me.

"Oh, right, sorry. I got distracted by the bling. So, we traced the email IP to the library. The library is closed on Sundays, so I'll swing by tomorrow and see if anyone remembers who was using the public computers at lunchtime on Thursday when the email was sent."

"Good work."

"I know." I picked up the last jewelry box and handed it to Galloway, only it slipped from my fingers and hit the floor, bouncing twice before the lid popped open. The bracelets it was holding spilled onto the carpet.

"Sorry, sorry." Dropping to my hands and knees, I carefully picked up the diamond-encrusted bracelets, terrified of breaking one. I was also conscious that I was kneeling next to the stained carpet where Gianna had died.

Gianna had no qualms, stepping on the dried pool of blood and pointing. "That one rolled away."

I retrieved the errant bracelet and put it in the box, about to hand it to Galloway when something caught my eye. "What's that?"

"What's what?" Gianna and Galloway both said.

"There." I pointed to a smudge of black on the bottom corner of the island bench. "That black stuff. What is it?"

Galloway took the bracelet box from me and secured it in the safe, locking the door and repositioning the portrait before squatting by my side to take a look.

"Grease, maybe?"

"How could there be grease in my dressing room?" Gianna stood over us. "My housekeeper cleans everything thoroughly, including wiping down this bench. She knows it has to be pristine in here. These clothes are haute couture. I can't have my Dior pants brushing against this and leaving a mark."

"She says her housekeeper cleans in here thoroughly."

"Wait here. I'm going to get a swab kit from the car."

"Looks like the cops missed it." Ben crossed his arms over his chest and rocked back on his heels.

"We would have too if I hadn't been down here on my hands and knees," I pointed out. "It practically blends in with the marble countertop." The countertop ran down both ends of the island bench in a waterfall design, dark swirls effectively disguising the smudge. For that was all it was, a small, dark smudge. Had the killer grabbed hold of the bench for balance after they'd stabbed Gianna? Crouched where I was kneeling, held onto the bench for balance, and pulled out the screwdriver.

"What are you thinking, Fitz?" Ben asked, watching me intently.

"I'm thinking we need to test Troy Barnes's hands for grease. He works on cars."

"Troy Barnes?" Gianna cut in. "He's no mechanic."

"Tell me what you know about him." I stood, my knees protesting from too long on the floor.

"I represented his wife, Elissa, in their divorce. Mind you, she wasn't much better."

"What do you mean?"

"Only that she had the good fortune to hire me first; otherwise, the shoe would be on the other foot.

They had a prenup. If either of them was caught cheating, kiss goodbye to anything in the subsequent divorce."

"Troy was cheating?"

"With some pet groomer. Michelle York. I believe he kept seeing her after the divorce, or so I've heard."

"What do you mean about the shoe being on the other foot?" Ben asked.

"Oh, Elissa was having an affair too. Only Troy was the one careless enough to get caught. Or get caught first. I think *that's* what's fueling his anger." Gianna looked from Ben to me. "I'm good at what I do, Audrey. I kept that information well and truly hidden from the court. It didn't come out until the divorce was final. And, of course, Troy is no fool. He knew he'd been played by Elissa, and there was nothing he could do about it."

"Except kill you."

"Yes, he was angry at me for defending his wife, but he was *furious* with her. If he was going to kill anyone, it would be Elissa."

Fair point. It was hardly Gianna's fault that she was good at her job. If Troy's lawyer had been half as good as Gianna, he'd have discovered Elissa's infidelity, and the outcome could have been very different. I turned to Ben. "Galloway is going to check traffic cams to verify Troy's alibi. He said he passed out drunk in his truck.

That means his truck must've been parked near The Bay somewhere."

"Let me guess—you want me to *do my thing*?" He waggled his fingers in the air with a devilish grin.

"Please."

"At your service."

I wish I could say he disappeared in a puff of smoke cos that would've been cool, but nope, he just disappeared. Not even a pop.

After Galloway had swabbed the grease mark, we turned out the lights and locked up the house. Gianna had declared she was *turning in for the night.* She still didn't have a handle on how this ghost thing worked, but if it gave her comfort to go through the motions of the living, who was I to burst her bubble?

13

*T*aking another huge bite of pizza, I waved the pink marker I was holding at the whiteboard in my office. "I still like Harry Watts for this," I mumbled through the melted cheese goodness in my mouth.

Galloway, who slouched in my office chair, chewed his pizza, head cocked to one side. "He's got an alibi. A solid one. He didn't kill Gianna Tate."

I tapped the marker against Harry's name, leaving pink dots behind. "How can he have signed a lease when he didn't have the money? That money had to have come from somewhere!" I sucked in a breath, taking with it a crumb of pizza, which caught in my windpipe, leaving me coughing and spluttering, my eyes streaming. Bent over double, I admired the charcoal grey tones of the carpet while my throat spasmed, and it crossed my mind how uncool it would be to be taken out by a pizza crumb.

Galloway thumped me on the back several times until I straightened, peering at him through blurry eyes. "I'm fine," I wheezed, reaching for my beer. "What if Watts is the blackmailer?" My voice sounded like I'd been chewing rusty nails, and I took another swig, trying to soothe my abused throat.

"But Gianna didn't pay, and the blackmailer failed to follow up with instructions on a money drop."

"You think they got cold feet?" I chewed the end of the marker, deep in thought. "They shoot off that email. Maybe something happened to prompt it, and they're all riled up. Angry. But later, when they've calmed down a bit, they realize what a dick move it was and abandon the plan."

"Which fits with Harry Watts's story. He was mad that Gianna held back from signing the loan documents."

"Yeah, but that was Saturday. The email was sent Thursday."

"Maybe the bank broke the news on Thursday? He got angry and fired off an email. But then he calmed down, knowing he was having lunch with Gianna on Saturday. Figured he'd hash it out with her then."

I went back to tapping the whiteboard. "But in the meantime, he's signing a lease?" I turned and wrote next to his name *'look into financials.'*

"Regardless, he's not our killer."

"Which brings us to Troy Barnes."

"Motive and opportunity." Galloway held out the pizza box, and I took another slice, sauce dripping on my shirt.

"I'm iffy on the opportunity. He says he was drunk and sleeping it off in his truck. The footage from The Bay certainly shows that he was under the influence. He was definitely angry at Gianna, threatening to kill her, which is pretty damming. But then, how would a drunk man be able to sneak into a party undetected?" I rubbed at the stain, spreading it.

"The party was loud, and everyone was in the ballroom. No one was watching the front door. Plus, Troy has a toolbox in the back of his truck. If I were to search it, I bet I'd find screwdrivers."

"Hardly a crime. You think he'd be stupid enough to stab his victim with a screwdriver and then put it back in his toolbox?" I wasn't buying it.

Galloway wasn't either, judging by the shake of his head. "Nah. I'd get rid of it."

"What about the grease we found in Gianna's dressing room? Gianna said that Troy isn't a mechanic. You said he works with cars, but he doesn't work *on* them. He sells them. What was his previous occupation? Before his life went to hell in a handbasket?"

Galloway pulled out his phone and began tapping,

swiping, and scrolling. "He was an investment broker," he eventually said.

Wow. I hadn't been expecting that. Troy Barnes had definitely hit rock bottom. From his scruffy appearance to his living situation, I'd never have guessed he'd been a bonafide, suit-wearing executive in his previous life.

"His divorce wiped him out. And clients quickly lose confidence in an advisor with no money."

"He has motive up the wazoo." But it niggled me. He was our top suspect, yet I wasn't convinced. If Troy was our man, how did he get in and out of Gianna's house undetected? He was drunk, meaning he would most likely stumble around, crash into things, cuss out loud. Someone would have seen or heard something. The fact that they hadn't had me circling Troy's name over and over on the whiteboard.

"Not convinced?" Galloway drew my attention to the fact I was scribbling on the board.

I quickly whipped my hands behind my back. "He looks good for it," I admitted. "But we have no evidence."

"Who else do we have?"

Chewing the inside of my cheek, I wrote one more name on the board, tapping it. "Chris Haiden. Attorney. He was pushing to be moved into Gianna's department. Family law. But they had no vacancies, so they kept telling him no."

"Not much of a motive."

I sighed, dejected. "I know." It was weak. I mean, would you really kill your boss over something so trivial? But that didn't mean I would rule him out as a blackmail suspect. I underlined his name and wrote '*blackmailer*?' It was flimsy, and I felt like I was clutching at straws, but Gianna herself had drawn my attention to him. "You're right. I don't think he's our killer. Which brings us back to these two."

"One. I told you. Harry Watts has a rock-solid alibi. He's on camera at his new gym when Gianna was killed."

Which meant Troy Barnes had to have killed Gianna Tate. We had no other options.

"We should look deeper into this whole blackmail thing. That has to be the key," Galloway said, breaking into my thoughts. Finishing his beer, he tugged me down to sit on his lap. "It's possible the blackmailer *is* the killer. Say Gianna turned the tables and told the blackmailer that she was going to the cops. They panicked, killed her to shut her up."

Looping my arms around his neck, I smiled. "Now, *that* is a theory I can get behind." Running my fingers through his hair, I thought back over the case. As far as I knew, Gianna hadn't responded to the blackmail threat, but what if she had? She'd *said* she was going to hire me, but the email came on Thursday. She was killed early Saturday evening. Plenty of time to give me a call, yet I hadn't heard from her until she turned up in her ghostly form. "She didn't mention responding to the threat."

"Lied by omission?" Galloway slid a warm hand up my back.

"That's the trouble with liars." I leaned down and kissed him. "They lie."

"You didn't tell me you got a warrant." I wasn't sure if I was annoyed or impressed that Galloway had managed to keep that little detail from me until now. He'd woken me with a kiss and a steaming cup of coffee, telling me to get my butt out of bed cos he had a warrant to search Gianna's office. If I wanted to go with him, then I'd better hustle.

I'd hustled. I'd shot out of bed so fast my foot had gotten tangled in the sheets, and I'd ended up in an undignified heap on the floor with Bandit rushing to sit on my chest to check on my wellbeing while Thor sat on the windowsill and looked on with disdain. Galloway had hauled me up and made sure I was steady on my feet before releasing his hold and repeating to get a move on.

Which was how I came to be standing beside him outside of Beasley, Tate, and Associates, wearing one faded blue Chuck and one yellow. I'd pulled on a pair of jeans I'd found on the floor and a clean T-shirt.

Right now, I was reasonably confident that a neglected pair of panties was bunched up in my right pant leg, slowly heading south.

"Ready?" Galloway asked, eyes sweeping over me.

"As I'll ever be." I just hoped Amanda wouldn't look at my feet. Or the panties didn't fall out of my pant leg at an inopportune moment.

"You look beautiful." Galloway read my mind. "Mis-matched shoes and all."

"I knew there was a reason I liked you." I slipped my hand into his and squeezed. I wasn't used to the compliments, but that wasn't to say I didn't enjoy them, and Galloway had apparently made it his mission to compliment me often.

Lifting our joined hands to his mouth, Galloway dropped a kiss on the back of mine before releasing it and pushing open the door. I followed behind, not too close as I was carrying a takeout coffee, and if I didn't notice he'd stopped, and I walked into him? Well, spilling this coffee would be sacrilegious.

"Detective Kade Galloway." His voice took on that authoritative ring that I liked so much, and I tried to school my face not to reveal my delight. "I have a search warrant for Gianna Tate's office."

I stepped to the side so I could see. Carolyn Wells sat behind the desk, her hair pulled into an elegant bun. Her makeup was understated except for the red lipstick, which suited her coloring perfectly. I touched my mouth, wondering if I could pull off such a shade. She wore a white button-down with a black blazer. The reception desk hid her lower half, but I imagined she was wearing a matching skirt and heels. Chic, elegant, professional. All the things I'm not. Still, I had a grande butter-pecan extra shot latte, and she didn't, so there's always that.

"One moment," she said.

Galloway glanced at me, and I shrugged.

"Sorry to interrupt, Felix, but the police are here with a search warrant," she said into the phone, her dulcet tones oddly soothing. I could see why Gianna wanted to keep her on reception, for despite the police turning up, with a search warrant no less, she wasn't rattled. She was calm and, above all else, professional.

Hanging up the phone, she smiled. "Please, take a seat. Felix will be with you shortly. Can I get you anything while you wait? Tea? Coffee?"

"We're good, thanks." Rather than sitting, Galloway cupped my elbow and led me across the foyer to stand near the window, the warrant in his hand.

A minute later, a man burst through the door separating the reception area from the rest of the building, an air of authority apparent in every move. His full head of gray hair was slicked back, his equally gray mustache neatly trimmed, and his gray and white pinstripe suit tailored perfectly, the jacket's cut helping disguise the dad bod beneath, the red handkerchief in the breast pocket a splash of color against his monochromatic appearance.

"Felix Beasley." He approached with his hand outstretched. "Please, come through."

Galloway accepted the handshake. "Detective Kade Galloway. This is Audrey Fitzgerald."

When Felix turned to me, I dutifully shook his hand, then—I have no idea why—executed an awkward bow curtsy-type affair that had me blushing deep red at my own gaucheness.

Felix didn't notice, turning his attention back to Galloway. "I hear you have a search warrant." It wasn't a question.

"Correct." Galloway held it out, and Felix took it without looking at it.

"Come on through."

We followed as he led us through the open-plan offices to Gianna's penthouse-style office. I kept my eyes on Felix's back, deliberately not looking toward Amanda's desk where, no doubt, she'd be desperately trying to get my attention. I had three missed calls from her already, and I knew it was either to press me for info on the investigation or hound me about the wedding.

Gianna was behind her desk, this time in a red power suit, complete with matching lipstick, and I was dying to know how she managed the wardrobe changes. No ghost I'd come across so far had been

able to do that. They all stayed in the outfit they'd
died in.

She glanced up when we entered. "Oh good, you're
here. I've got court this morning, but it shouldn't take
long." She addressed Felix. "The Harris case. Open and
shut, so I expect to be back within the hour." She
stood, shoving a bunch of files into her briefcase and
snapping it shut. "We still on for our one o'clock this
afternoon?" She shot a glance at the Tag Heuer watch
adorning her wrist.

Totally ignoring Galloway and me, she stepped
around the desk and walked past us, patting Felix on
the shoulder as she did so, apparently not noticing that
he hadn't responded to her. "Good, good. I'll see you
then." And she left. Presumably, off to court.

"Everything okay?" Galloway said into my ear.

"What?" I realized I'd turned to watch Gianna leave
and was now facing the door. "Yeah, yeah, all good.
Sorry." I cleared my throat. "Nice office."

Felix ignored us and opened the warrant, perusing
the contents.

"This looks fine," he said, folding it and sliding it
inside his jacket pocket. Galloway's lips twitched, but
he didn't comment. It didn't matter if Felix approved of
the warrant or not. It was a legal document giving us
access to Gianna's client files and anything else of
interest in her office.

"We'll need the passwords to her computer," Galloway said, moving behind Gianna's desk.

"I'll send in Jessica, her paralegal. She can walk you through anything you need."

"Wasn't Gianna due in court today?" I asked, and Felix shot me a look, his eyes narrowing. "How did you know that?"

"I'm a PI. It's my job to know." Oh my God, cheesiest line in history, but it worked. Felix totally bought it.

"Jack has taken over the case. He'll be representing Gianna's client."

"Which case is that?" Galloway asked.

"June Harris versus Adam Harris."

"Divorce," I added for Galloway's benefit. I already knew all about the case directly from Gianna. June Harris was going for custody of the couple's dog. I would have thought it was hardly worthy of the judge's time, but divorcing couples never ceased to amaze me with the lengths they'd go to inflict pain on their former spouse.

Felix headed to the door, pausing to shoot us a look over his shoulder. "Jessica will be in shortly. Please, if you need anything, let me know. We fully intend to cooperate and get to the bottom of Gianna's murder."

"Good to know." Galloway inclined his head, and the door softly shut behind Felix's retreating back.

Placing my coffee on Gianna's desk, I vetoed the

uncomfortable barrel chairs and opted for standing, rubbing my hands together. "Right, what's first?"

"First, you tell me if Gianna is here."

"Not anymore. She was when we first arrived. She's gone to court."

Galloway's brows lowered. "Court?"

"Mmmm. Seems she's regressed into thinking she's still alive. Which is odd. I've never dealt with a ghost quite like Gianna before."

"Oh?"

"For one, she can change clothes. And she can—I don't know what you'd call it—fashion real-life items but in spirit form."

"What do you mean?" Galloway began opening drawers on Gianna's desk and poking around inside. I was glad she wasn't here. She'd probably have a conniption at the invasion of privacy.

"Well, she conjured up some files and a briefcase. That type of thing. Gianna is sometimes in some sort of alternate reality where she believes she's alive and is going about her day-to-day business. She doesn't notice that people don't respond to her. She didn't acknowledge me at all this morning."

"Is Ben around?"

I shook my head. "Nope. I haven't seen him today."

"Never mind, we'll just have to do this the old-fashioned way." Taking a seat in Gianna's scrumptious chair, he paused, patted the arms, wriggled his butt, and muttered, "Nice chair."

I wanted to say, "I know, right?" but that would give away that I'd been here before. It wouldn't take a genius to work out that Ben and I had broken into Gianna's office. Galloway wouldn't appreciate that little bit of news, so I kept my mouth shut.

He wriggled the mouse, and the monitor came to life, making me frown. When we were here yesterday, I distinctly remember turning the computer off. Had someone else been snooping?

"Hi, guys, I'm Jessica." The door opened, and a blonde, curly head popped in. "Can I get y'all a coffee before we get started?" Jessica Watson had a remarkable similarity to Marilyn Monroe. No wonder she'd chosen that as her costume for the Scarecrow Ball. With her loose platinum curls bouncing around her head, black-winged eyeliner, and pink lips, she bore more than a passing resemblance to the star. She was dressed in black pants, stilettoes, and a pale pink button-down, the cuffs turned up, exuding an image of casual elegance. I sighed, glancing down at my mismatched shoes.

"Not for me," Galloway said. "Audrey?"

"I've already got one, but thank you." I picked up the take-out cup and took a sip.

Jessica stepped fully into the room, closing the

door behind her. "All right then, what can I do to help?"

"You can unlock Gianna's computer for a start." Galloway rolled the chair back, giving Jessica space. While they did that, I meandered over to the row of filing cabinets at the back of the room. There were six of them, white with brass handles and a highly polished and glossed slab of wood across the top, effectively creating a benchtop out of the row of cabinets. Clever.

"What's in these? Client files?"

Jessica glanced up from where she was typing in Gianna's password. "Only current client files. The rest go to archives. Much of it is administration of this place, personnel, insurance, that type of thing."

I began opening the drawers and pawing my way through. Nothing jumped out at me. "Who has access to these? I notice they have locks, but they're all unlocked."

"Chloe locks them every night and unlocks them every morning. She does it for all the filing cabinets in the building. Felix has his own set, similar to Gianna's, and each of us has a lockable cabinet at our desks. Chloe has the master key."

"I also noticed Gianna's computer is on. Does she leave it on all the time?" I was quietly proud of how I'd segued to the computer being on without giving away my recent break and enter.

Jessica shook her head. "I turned it on this morning. Pure habit, I'm afraid." Her mouth drooped. "Gianna likes to get in early on court days, so I make sure I arrive before her and have everything ready."

"Which is?" Galloway asked.

"Computer on, unlock Gianna's filing cabinets if Chloe isn't in yet, coffee machine on. I'll also get out her planner and set it up on her desk."

The blotter on Gianna's desk was empty of any physical planner. "Her planner isn't here," Galloway pointed out.

"Sorry. It's on my desk. I was going through it, making sure I canceled or re-distributed any of her appointments."

"Doesn't she have an electronic calendar for that?" I should know. Ben accessed it for me.

"She does, but Gianna puts a lot of personal stuff in her physical planner. I just block out the time on her electronic one. It's my job to cross-reference them. Gianna often schedules appointments and forgets to transfer them across."

"We're going to need that day planner, Jessica," Galloway told her, and she nodded, her curls bouncing.

"Sure, I'll grab it now. Is it okay if I photocopy the next couple of weeks? I need to notify people of the...." She cleared her throat. "Change in circumstances."

"Sure."

While Jessica left to take care of the planner, I hunted for the personnel files, crowing in triumph when I found them.

"What are you up to?" Galloway asked as he scrolled through the files on the computer.

"I wanted to check my theory that Carolyn, the receptionist, was passed over for the office manager role that Chloe was hired for."

"And?"

"And hang on, I'm reading." I'd found Chloe's file and Carolyn's and all of the applications for the position. Spreading the papers across the workbench, I rifled through them. No application from Carolyn. Picking up her personnel file, I flicked through, looking for any mention of a promotion or at least a note to say Carolyn was interested in the office manager role. No such note existed. Carolyn hadn't applied, which blew my theory that she was passed over for a promotion out of the water.

"Nothing. There's nothing here." I put the files away. "How about you?"

"I'm looking at her online calendar, and I have to say that she doesn't have many clients for a high-ranking attorney. In fact, court this morning is all she has for this week."

"Really?" I hustled to peer over his shoulder. It was true. There was a staff meeting, a reminder that she had to write a piece for the Law Society newsletter, and then nothing. "How odd."

Jessica returned with Gianna's planner, a rose gold compendium with a gold zip and clasp. She placed it on the desk in front of Galloway. "Here you go."

Galloway jerked his thumb toward the monitor. "Have you moved most of Gianna's appointments out of her calendar?"

Jessica chewed her lip and looked toward the bookcase on her left before bringing her attention back to Galloway. "No." Something was up. That quick glance gave her away.

"Why does she have so few appointments?" I asked. "She's known in the business as a cut-throat divorce attorney. I would have thought she'd be booked solid."

"She used to be."

"Until?" Galloway unzipped the compendium and opened the planner.

Jessica drew in a deep breath and released it with a long sigh. "She didn't say. About three months ago, she called me in here and asked me to hand over most of her clients to Jack."

"But not the Harris case?"

"Yeah, that struck me as odd too. Ordinarily, Gianna wouldn't touch such a trivial case, but she seemed to get a kick out of it. Today would have been the first time she'd been in court for months."

I glanced at Galloway to get his take on this turn of

events. "What do you think?" I murmured. "You think she was winding down?"

"Getting ready to retire, maybe?"

Jessica overheard us. "She never mentioned retiring. Not to Felix and not to me."

I realized a lot was going on in Gianna Tate's life that she hadn't told me. Lies by omission. A surge of irritation shot through me, making my skin itch. I'd liked the woman; now I had the feeling she'd been playing me, and let's face it, an attorney of Gianna's caliber certainly had the skills to pull off any deception she wanted.

"Thanks, Jessica, you can go now. We'll yell out if we need anything further."

She nodded, spun on a heel, and left.

"You'll need to teach your face to use its inside voice," Galloway teased. "Obviously, you think Gianna was up to something. Something that got her killed. Care to share?"

A flush of heat washed over my cheeks at being called out. "That's just it," I said, fanning my face. "All I have is this *feeling* that Gianna has intentionally led me astray."

Galloway's phone rang. I listened to the one-sided conversation, knowing I wouldn't like the news when he kept shooting me the side-eye.

"What?" I snapped when he hung up.

"Troy Barnes's alibi holds."

I began pacing. "Of course it does."

"We've got his truck on a traffic camera. The image is grainy, but you can see him reclining in the driver's seat. He didn't leave until two in the morning."

"Meaning he couldn't have killed Gianna."

Galloway slapped his hands on the desktop and pushed to his feet. "Yup. Come on, let's tear this place apart. She was hiding something. Something that got her killed."

14

We found nothing. Zip, zilch, nada. The only exciting thing was that my wadded-up panties finally made a bid for freedom, working their way out the bottom of the leg of my jeans. I tripped over them, resulting in a face plant on Gianna's plush office carpet.

Galloway hurried to help me up. "You okay? What happened? *Are those your panties*?"

I rolled over and lay on my back, staring up at him. "Would you be surprised if I said they were?"

"Not at all. Come on." He held out a hand and hauled me to my feet, tugging me into an embrace.

"Thanks," I mumbled into his chest, sliding my arms around his waist.

"I've got to get these files back to the station and have the team go through them with a fine-tooth comb." His voice rumbled beneath my ear. The files he was talking about were Gianna's most recent cases, dating back a year, stacked inside an archive box, her day planner on top.

"I'm going to the library to see if we can't track down this blackmailer," I said. On the one hand, I was relieved we hadn't found anything concrete during the search. It meant I hadn't done such a terrible job the first time around. But on the other hand, it sucked. We were no closer to finding her killer or blackmailer. Instead, we'd unearthed more questions than we had answers for.

Releasing me from the embrace, Galloway dropped an absent-minded kiss on my cheek and scooped up the panties, shoving them in his pocket. "Keep me posted."

"Will do."

While he gathered the coffee cups we'd used during our three hours of searching to return them to the kitchen, I swiped Gianna's planner, and I didn't even feel bad about it. Shoving it into my tote bag, I quickly put the lid back on the archive box, tossed my bag over my shoulder, and picked up the box. I met Galloway at the door, holding it out to him. "Here you go."

"Thanks." My luck held. He didn't notice the box was lighter than it should have been.

We'd had the foresight to bring separate cars, and I

waited in mine until Galloway had pulled away before closing my eyes and thinking about Ben. Summoning him, if you like.

He popped into the passenger seat a moment later. "You called?"

"I'm heading to the library. I figured we could have another crack at tracking down Gianna's blackmailer. Have you seen her today?"

"Nah, I figured she was at her office, but I'm assuming not if you were just there."

"She was here when we first arrived, then said she had court, but that was three hours ago, and she hasn't returned."

"Maybe court is still going."

I shrugged. "Could be. She thought it was an open and shut case and expected to be done within an hour."

"Okay, well, let's go to the library first, and then I'll head over to the courthouse, see what's happening."

"That'll work, thanks."

This time when I pulled into the library parking lot, spaces were scarce. I lapped the lot twice before snagging a spot in the back. Heaving my tote bag over my shoulder, I hurried inside, stopping by the information desk while Ben headed straight for the bank of computers available for the public to use.

"Good afternoon. How may I help you?" I don't know why I pictured Mrs. Doubtfire as how a librarian should look, but the young kid before me with the pimply face and gaucheness of youth was not what I expected.

"Oh." I cleared my throat, caught off guard. "Can I speak to someone in charge?"

"Regarding?" the twelve-year-old said. Okay, fine, he probably wasn't twelve—child labor laws wouldn't allow it—but he *looked* twelve.

"I'm a private investigator—" I began, only to have him cut me off.

"You are? Cool! Do you have a badge?" His eyes rounded, and his mouth opened in an O. "Or a gun?"

I dug around in my tote. "I have a business card," I deadpanned, handing him one.

He took it and examined it closely. "Delaney Investigations," he read out loud. "But your surname is Fitzgerald. Why not Fitzgerald Investigations? Or is Delaney your boss?"

"Ben Delaney started the business, and I took it over when he died. I kept the name." Why was I explaining myself to this kid? I cleared my throat and began again. "Anyway, I'm investigating Gianna Tate's murder. You may have heard about it? On the news?"

"Oh, yeah. I did. Some rich, old lady bit the big one in her mansion."

I blinked. *Would we call her old?* Ignoring that, I pressed on. "We think someone sent her an email from one of the computers here."

The twelve-year-old glanced over at the computers in question where Ben was doing the rounds, placing his hand on each one and scanning the metadata.

"Okaaaay?" He turned his attention back to me. "But we don't track what people send. We don't record what they do on those computers."

"No, I get that," I assured him. "But I wondered if you recall who was in here Thursday lunchtime."

The twelve-year-old threw back his head and laughed like I'd told the best joke in the world. I tapped my foot, waiting for him to get his mirth under control. Eventually, he did, rubbing his eyes with his fists.

"Oh man, that's gold," he sniggered, then caught sight of my not amused expression. "So, yeah, that'd be a no. As you can see, we have six available for public use, and people use them—a lot. We have another four in that room," he pointed, "but you have to have a library card to access those. Your login information is recorded."

"Who uses those?"

"Mostly college students. It's quieter in the room, plus you can book a computer, so you know when you come to study that you'll have access, whereas the public ones, you just have to take a gamble that one will be free."

"And I'm assuming no CCTV?" I glanced around, not spotting any cameras.

"No, ma'am."

"Okay, well, thanks for your time." Ben had finished with the computers and was headed my way, lifting his arms in a no-luck gesture.

"Wait." The twelve-year-old stopped me as I turned away by grabbing my arm. I shot him a look, and he quickly removed his hand. "How did she die? The old lady."

"Firstly, she was hardly old. She was fifty-five, and these days, that's only half your expected lifetime." Give or take. "And she was stabbed. Why? Do you know something?"

He shook his head. "Nah. Just wondered, is all."

"Well, thanks for your help...." I trailed off, waiting for him to supply his name.

"Bryce."

"Thanks for your help, Bryce. You have a good day now."

"No help?" Ben guessed, falling into step beside me as I headed for the exit. Which was when I had an idea. Spinning, I retraced my steps, whispering to Ben out the corner of my mouth, "There's another room with four computers over there on our left. Only library members can use them."

"On it."

"Back so soon?" Bryce asked with a smile. Pulling out my phone, I held up a photo of Gianna. "This is the lady who died. Has she been in here recently?"

He shook his head. "Nope."

I showed him photos of each Beasley, Tate, and Associates staff member and got the same response. That is, until Carolyn Wells.

"Oh, yeah, she comes in here all the time."

"She does?"

"Yeah." He nodded. "She doesn't use the computers, though. She borrows books. Lady likes to read, like, a lot!"

"Oh." Darn. I thought I had a lead. I showed him a photo of Troy Barnes and Harry Watts in one last-ditch effort.

"Sorry." Bryce shrugged. "Guess they're not your killer, huh?"

"Thanks again. You've been a great help." I forced a smile and returned to the car, waiting for Ben, who appeared a few minutes later.

"You're not going to believe this." His level of excitement told me he'd found something juicy.

"What did you find?"

"Only that June Harris is a library member, and she was booked to use one of those computers on Thursday from twelve until one."

"June Harris," I repeated. "The same June Harris who Gianna is representing in court? Today?"

"One and the same." Ben nodded, practically bouncing in his seat. "So? What are you waiting for? Let's go!"

I started the engine and pulled out of the lot, heading for the courthouse. "Could you tell if the email was sent from that computer?" I asked Ben as I drove.

"Yep. I was able to get into the email account. It was the only email that was sent. Ever."

"Did Gianna reply?" Despite her telling me she hadn't, I wasn't sure I could trust her anymore.

"Nope. No activity other than that one sent email."

Weird. Why would June Harris attempt to blackmail her own lawyer?

"What are you talking about?" June Harris had hold of her dog's collar, who was barking up a storm at my knocking on her front door. When we'd arrived at the courthouse, we discovered the Harris case was well and truly over, and the court had recessed for lunch. I figured June would be at home, celebrating her win or mourning her loss.

"I'm talking about you using one of the Firefly Bay Library's computers last Thursday to send an email to Gianna Tate, attempting to blackmail her."

The dog, a black pug, would not stop whining and crying, so June opened the door wider and beckoned me inside. "You'd better come in. He's not going to stop."

"Nice dog. I take it you won?" June was still in her court clothes, a neatly pressed black suit, now adorned with dog hair.

Releasing her hold on the dog caught in the middle of all this, she watched as said dog thoroughly sniffed my shoes.

"I guess." She shrugged. "I won custody but with visitation rights. Adam gets him one weeknight and every second weekend."

"You both must really love him. What's his name?"

"Prince."

"So, tell me, June, why were you blackmailing your own lawyer?"

Ben, who'd been trying to get Prince's attention—and failing—finally gave up and pointed to the passageway leading off the living room, indicating he was going to snoop around. I disguised my nod by rubbing my hand around the nape of my neck.

"That's the most ridiculous thing I've ever heard. Why on Earth would you think I'd do such a thing? I didn't need to blackmail Gianna. I was one hundred percent confident she'd win my case."

"Because a threatening email was sent to her from one of the library computers. A computer booked under your name, using your library card."

Her mouth dropped open, and her hand flew to her throat. "What? That's not possible. I haven't been to the library in ages, let alone used one of their computers. Why would I? I have a laptop here." She pointed to the laptop sitting on her coffee table.

"To hide the fact that the email came from you."

"But it didn't!"

"Prove it," I challenged.

Her arms dropped to her sides, and her hands clenched into fists before relaxing. "Why that dirty little weasel. I knew he was low, but I never thought him capable of something like this," she hissed.

It didn't take a genius to figure out she was referring to her now ex-husband, Adam Harris.

"Adam doesn't have a library membership. I do." She dashed out of the room, and I followed her into her kitchen, where her handbag sat on the counter. Digging around for her purse, she pulled it out, then rifled through it. She held it out to me, pointing to an empty card slot. "See that? That's where my library card lives. He stole it. He stole my library card and used it to try and implicate me in a crime. Arrest him!"

I held up both hands in a pacifying gesture. "Firstly, I can't arrest him. I'm a PI, not a cop. And secondly, we need proof that your ex took the card and not someone else."

"Who else could it be?" Sarcasm dripped from every word, and I didn't blame her. It certainly looked like Adam Harris had taken his wife's library card to use a computer at the library to send the blackmail email. I gazed out the window above June's sink, lost in thought. Did he think he could blackmail Gianna into throwing the case? Drop June as a client, so he'd win custody of Prince? It was so farfetched it just might be true.

"Now what?" June asked.

"I'll speak with Adam, and if I can dig up enough proof that he did this, I'll be turning it over to the police. Blackmail is a criminal offense; charges may be pressed."

I didn't add that maybe Adam had killed Gianna in a desperate bid to keep his dog.

15

While I waited in my car for Ben to finish snooping in June's house, I opened my PI app and typed in Adam Harris, narrowing the search results to Firefly Bay. Bingo. One result, and according to the app, Adam had no criminal history. He worked retail in a popular men's clothing store on Main Street, and his new address since he'd moved out of the marital home was an apartment on Grave Avenue.

"Nothing terribly exciting to report." Ben materialized in the passenger seat, causing my heart to skip a beat. Even though I was expecting him, the way he popped in and out still startled me. "That dog has more toys than I did throughout my entire childhood. And June has a valium prescription. Other than that..."

"I don't think she's our blackmailer anyway. Her

library card is missing, and she's pointing the finger at Adam."

"Plausible. Unless she dropped it, and someone picked it up."

"It has its own slot in her purse. It's not the type of thing you'd just drop without noticing. You'd have had to have taken it out of your purse in the first place, but I appreciate you playing devil's advocate. Hypothetically, what are the chances that June did drop it and some random picked it up and thought, *'You know what? I'm going to use this to send a blackmail email to a high-profile lawyer.'*"

"Point taken. So. Adam's place?"

"Adam's place," I agreed.

The great thing about living in Firefly Bay? It literally takes you minutes to get from point A to point B. Granted, Adam now lived across town from June, but across town wasn't that far, and a scant ten minutes later, I was knocking on the door of apartment 2B.

The door flung open. "What?"

I eyeballed the disheveled blond standing in front of me in boxers and a T-shirt, a bottle of beer clutched in one hand, the other holding the door. Or maybe the door was holding him up?

"Adam Harris?"

"Who wants to know?" He leaned toward me, peering intently into my face, and the wave of alcohol on his breath almost knocked me down. Putting a hand on his chest, I pushed him away. "Back up a step, bud. You might want to take it easy on those." I indicated the bottle he had half raised to his mouth.

"Who are you? My mother? Or worse, my wife?" He snorted, then laughed, turning away and leaving the door open. I took it as an invitation and stepped inside. Seemed like Adam was drowning his losses. Tossed over the back of the sofa was a suit jacket. On the floor were the matching pants. The coffee table was littered with beer bottles.

"Pity party for one," I said under my breath.

"I'll look around." Ben left me with the intoxicated Adam Harris. This was either going to be incredibly easy or incredibly difficult.

"Having a bad day, Adam?"

"I've had better." He slouched on the sofa, watching me. "Who'd you say you were again?"

"Audrey Fitzgerald. PI."

"PI?"

"Private investigator."

"That's a real thing?" He guffawed, leaning forward to slap his thighs. I failed to see what was so funny, but whatever.

"Very real," I assured him. "I'm here to ask you about Gianna Tate."

"June's lawyer? What about her?" Picking at the label on his beer bottle, he refused to look at me.

"Why were you trying to blackmail her?"

"Ouch," Ben said from behind me. "Straight for the jugular."

Adam didn't reply immediately. He just kept picking at the label. "Who says I was trying to blackmail her?"

"Oh, he's our man." Ben slapped me on the back, causing my shoulder blades to temporarily freeze on impact. I gritted my teeth and tried not to react. "There's nothing much here," he continued. "Old Adam is a bit of a minimalist. Or he's broke thanks to his divorce, and he can't afford anything beyond the basics."

A quick perusal of my surroundings had me agreeing with Ben's assessment. Aside from the sofa, coffee table, and television, there was nothing else in the living room. No knickknacks, no soft furnishings. Just the essentials.

"Computer?" I asked out of the corner of my mouth.

"Not that I can find."

Picking up Adam's pants from the floor, I dug around in the pockets, pulling out his wallet.

"Hey!" Adam protested. "What are you doing?"

Ignoring him, I flipped it open, and there, shoved in with a credit card, was June Harris's library card. I held it up, tossing the wallet to Adam, who failed to catch it, and it bounced off his chest onto the floor.

"Care to tell me what you were doing in the library at lunchtime Thursday?" I asked, waggling the card.

"That's not mine," he declared defensively.

"I know it's not. You swiped it from your wife. To implicate her in your blackmail scheme."

He still wouldn't look at me. Instead, he examined his sock-clad feet, lips clamped shut.

"Let me tell you how I think it went down, and you can tell me I'm right." I paced, tapping the library card in my hand. "You knew you were going to lose the court case against June, that she would win custody of Prince. So, you hatched a desperate plan. Blackmail her lawyer. I'm not sure why you thought that would be a good idea because it wouldn't stop her from taking the case—after all, if your blackmail letter mentioned this case, she'd know it was you. So, you figured, what, a hundred grand should cover your pain and suffering? You could set yourself up in your new life. Get a new dog. Maybe some furniture."

Adam's face paled, and I wondered if he was going to pass out. Or puke. Either way, I was on the right track. "Then what happened, Adam? She didn't give in to your demands, and you lost your cool and killed her?"

"No!" He shot to his feet, the clunk of the beer bottle hitting the floor and the slosh of liquid spilling loud in the silent apartment. "That's not what happened. I didn't kill her, I swear."

"But you did attempt to blackmail her."

He threw up his hands. "Yes. Yes, okay, fine, I admit it. It was me. But I did not kill her, I swear." He sniffed, his eyes tearing up. "I'm such a screw-up. A failure. I didn't even have the balls to follow through on the blackmail thing." He sat back down, cradling his head in his hands, and sobbed.

I looked at Ben, horrified. "Now what?" I whispered.

Ben looked as uncomfortable as I felt. "I guess we take him to the station?"

"A citizen's arrest?" I chewed my lip, considering my options. "I'm calling Galloway."

While Adam continued to cry like a broken man, I dialed my one and only, beyond relieved when he picked up on the second ring.

"Hey, babe, listen, I'm at Adam Harris's apartment, and he's confessed to the blackmail attempt on Gianna."

Adam stopped crying and lifted his head, cheeks wet with tears, snot all over his top lip. Reaching into my tote, I dug out a tissue and tossed it to him.

"I'll have him picked up. What led you to him?"

I told him about my trip to the library, the recording of June's library card accessing one of the computers when the email was sent, the visit to June, and the subsequent discovery that her library card was missing, which ultimately led me to Adam's door.

"Sounds like he has a motive for murder," Galloway said.

"He says not."

"But what do you think?" he pressed, and I glanced at the distraught man on the sofa. Capable of murder? Isn't everyone? If you're backed into a corner, desperate, would you kill? If I was at risk of losing Thor and Bandit, I'd lay my life on the line for them, but was I prepared to take someone else's? In the heat of the moment... possibly. Premeditated? No.

"I've found no evidence of the weapon used to kill Gianna," Ben told me.

"It doesn't matter what I think," I eventually replied to Galloway. "It's the evidence that counts."

Galloway chuckled. "You should be a cop."

"Wash your mouth out," I teased. When I first met Galloway, it was no secret that I had a deep-seated distrust of law enforcement. Despite Ben once being on the force, the way he'd been framed and forced out of the profession he'd loved had hurt me as much as it had him, and I'd carried those hurts with me after he'd died. We probably wouldn't be talking wedding bells today if Galloway hadn't won me over by arresting the corrupt cops responsible.

"Officers Walsh and Collier are on patrol. I'll send them your way to pick him up."

"And search the place? You know, for the murder weapon."

"I'm assuming you've already done that, but yes, the Firefly Bay Police Department must cross their t's and dot their i's. Sergeant Young will take care of it."

"You're not coming?"

"I'll interview Harris at the station."

"You may have to wait 'til he sobers up." I glanced at the inebriated, emotional man on the sofa, who looked like someone had just kicked his puppy. I guess, in a way, they had.

Galloway sighed. "Thanks for the heads up. We'll put him in holding until he's sober. Can't muddy the waters of the investigation by interviewing a suspect under the influence of alcohol."

And *that* is why I love Detective Kade Galloway. That and other things, but his moral compass is sound, and I find that highly attractive. Bent cops like Officer Ian Mills would have most certainly interviewed Adam while he was drunk and taken and used that testimony to fit whatever crime they wanted it to fit.

I ended the call with Galloway, tossing Adam's pants to him. "You might want to put those on. The cops are on their way."

"To arrest me?"

I shrugged. "Probably take you in for questioning first. Trust me, just tell the truth. It'll work out better for you rather than lying." I'd like to say he'd be fine, but I wasn't sure he would be. He'd attempted to extort money from Gianna. That's illegal. But Gianna hadn't

—couldn't—press charges, so where that left Adam, I didn't know.

"I don't think he killed her," Ben said, watching Adam fumble around trying to dress.

"I don't either." But I had nothing concrete to back it up other than a gut feeling. I felt a little bit sorry for Adam, which was clouding my judgment. It wasn't Gianna's fault his marriage had collapsed. Still, the division of assets—particularly one pug dog named Prince—could be squarely placed at her door. But it was a catch twenty-two, for killing Gianna wouldn't stop the case from going to court. Another lawyer would be—and was—appointed, and Adam *still* lost the case.

"Who're you talking to?" Adam asked, standing to zip his pants.

"No one. Just myself."

"June used to do that. Talk to herself." And then he started crying again.

"He's a wreck," Ben said, then turned to the door. "Company's here."

A second later, there was a knock.

"I'll get it," I said to Adam, who was currently searching for his shoes. I opened the door to find Officers Collier and Walsh on the other side.

"Audrey." Tom Collier smiled and nodded in greeting.

"Hey, guys, come on in. Adam's just getting

dressed."

"Dressed? He was naked?" Noah Walsh exclaimed, slapping me on the shoulder as he walked past.

"Semi. He was in his boxers when I got here."

"Right. Galloway said we're to take him to the tank to sober up first."

"He's all yours." I left Adam with them and headed out, somehow losing Ben in the process. He'd either decided to stay behind with Tom and Noah or gone somewhere else, so the ride home was solo. I could have used our mysterious connection to summon him to me, but I didn't like to do that unless I actually needed his help with something. I can't imagine how annoying it would be for someone to have that type of power over you, to be able to pull you away from whatever it was you were doing without your consent.

16

On the whiteboard in my home office, I wrote Adam's name just to have the satisfaction of crossing it off and writing blackmailer next to it. Technically, I'd done what Gianna had hired me for— or had been about to hire me for—and that was to find her blackmailer. Now I just needed to find her killer.

Thor padded into the room, winding his way around my ankles. I bent down and scooped him into my arms, groaning at the weight. He really was one plump puss.

"How are you doing, hmmm?" I murmured, stroking my hand through his thick, lush fur. His purr was loud, vibrating against my chest.

"Okay, that's enough. Put me down," he demanded.

Shaking my head, I obliged. "Where's Bandit?"

"Asleep under the covers on your bed."

"I'll check on her in a minute." I don't know why I bothered telling him that, for his tailed swished as he headed out the room with an absent, "Whatever."

After staring at the whiteboard for five minutes with no clues jumping out, I headed to the kitchen and the nirvana that coffee provided. That's when I saw a note stuck on the glass sliding door. Opening the door, I plucked off the note. It was a postcard ad for a bridal expo in the city. On it, Seb had written, "We're going to this!"

Tossing the card onto the kitchen counter, I fixed myself a coffee. Hiring Seb as my wedding planner was meant to make my life easier. I sincerely hoped I hadn't created a monster. But he would, at least, create a nice buffer between Amanda and me.

"Mom!" Bandit hurtled down the stairs and skidded across the floor at full speed. The paw print pattern on her back was cute, but I must admit I preferred her with all her fur.

"Hey, Bandit." I scratched the top of her head and behind her ears, and she made a chittering sound of delight. Smiling, I gave her one last pat, turned, and that's when I noticed the pantry door ajar. The pantry door that I had doubly, triply checked was securely closed the night before.

"What's this?" I asked both Thor and Bandit.

Neither replied, which was odd as Thor was usually the first to protest his innocence and Bandit to proclaim she was sorry—whether she was guilty or not.

Opening the door, I flicked on the light, expecting to find a God-awful mess. What I found was Gianna, hand in my one remaining Cheez-It box, a guilty look on her face.

"Care to explain?" I asked, the scratch marks on my forehead starting to itch again.

"My one guilty pleasure," she admitted, removing her hand and wiping her palms on her rear.

"You lectured me about eating them." I was outraged. She'd dissed my love of junk food when all along... wait a minute. "Was it you? Did you let Bandit and Thor into the pantry? Showed them where I'd hidden the Cheez-Its?" I'd bought three boxes from Nick's Bodega cos they were on special. I'd intentionally hidden them because I knew Thor and Bandit would be all over it. I mean, come on, junk food and a trash panda?

"I did not!" Gianna declared, planting her hands on her hips. "What a ludicrous idea. I didn't even know you had these until I saw you shoving them in your face in your car!"

Fair point. "Okay, fine. Well, out you come. This door is meant to be closed to keep these two out." I jerked my thumb, and Gianna dutifully left the pantry. "How did you get the door open anyway?"

"The usual way." She sniffed. "By turning the handle."

"Yes, but ghosts can't physically touch things."

"The evidence clearly shows differently."

"I'm *clearly* going to have to install a lock."

After retrieving my coffee, I grabbed my tote bag and settled on the sofa, rummaging for Gianna's planner. Gianna took a seat in an armchair, watching me.

"So, tell me," I said conversationally. "Why so few clients over the last several months?"

Her brow furrowed. "What do you mean?"

"The last few months, you've only had one case. June Harris. How come? Were you planning on retiring?"

She reared back as if I'd slapped her. "Retiring? I'm fifty-five! Why would I retire?"

"I don't know, maybe because you could afford to? Maybe you were tired of working and wanted to travel? There's a host of reasons why you might want to retire."

She rubbed at her temple. "I'm not sure."

"You're not sure you were retiring? Or you're not sure why you stopped taking on clients?"

Her frown deepened. "I'm not sure I remember."

I sighed. So, we were back to that. Gianna's memory of her death was like Swiss cheese. Full of holes.

"Well," I held up the planner, "maybe the answer is in here."

"That's mine."

"Correct. And I'm hoping to find some clue as to who might have wanted you dead."

"I didn't want to die."

It was my turn to frown. "None of us do. But don't worry, between Galloway and me, we'll find out who did it. Justice will be done."

She nodded. "Justice. Yes." And then she disappeared.

"That was weird," I said to thin air before taking a sip of scalding coffee and flicking through the pages of her planner. Nothing noted on the Thursday she'd received the blackmail email, but she'd written '*hire Audrey*' on the Friday slot. So, she had intended to hire me, she just hadn't gotten around to calling, and then she'd been killed. I wondered if she'd made that call sooner, would she still be alive today?

Aside from regular hair, nail, and facial appointments, Gianna had blocked out a half-day every month where she'd written '*city*.' "Not helpful, Gianna." Obviously, she had a meeting in the city, but with whom, and why did it take half a day? My head snapped up, a thought occurring. "Where's your phone?" Her phone would tell me so much, like who she called when she was in the city. Maybe even photos of whatever it was she was getting up to.

Shooting off a text to Galloway, I asked, "Do the police have Gianna's phone?"

Eventually, he messaged back. "Negative."

How had I missed this? Gianna's phone was missing, which meant the killer had probably taken it. Which also meant there was something incriminating on the phone they didn't want the police to find. Of course, I was sure Galloway was subpoenaing her phone records. Still, as a PI, I could use my various apps and databases to, let's not say hack but *access* that information without all the red tape. Jumping up, I tossed the planner onto the coffee table, where it promptly slid across the surface and fell to the floor on the other side.

Bending to pick it up, I noticed a business card had come loose and was lying face down on the rug. Something was written on the back. Picking it up, I took a closer look. It was a date and a time. Flipping it over, I read Bradley Howard, attorney, Sante Law.

Grabbing the planner, I flipped through the pages, matching up the date Gianna had written on the back. And there it was. Gianna was in the city that day to meet with another law firm. Did she intend to leave

Firefly Bay? Not retire but relocate, work for another law firm?

Hurrying into my office, I woke up the computer and began typing. Once I'd gained entry to Gianna's phone records, it wasn't difficult to match up the number on the business card. Gianna had spoken with Bradley Howard frequently. Almost too often to be considered a job interview, I would have thought, but then I didn't know the hiring process for an attorney of Gianna's caliber. Maybe it was more robust than the standard I was used to. The only way to find out what it was regarding was to talk to the lawyer myself.

"Bradley Howard." The British accent on the other end of the line threw me. It reminded me so much of Thor. "Hello?" he prompted when I didn't immediately respond.

"Sorry." I cleared my throat. "My name is Audrey Fitzgerald. I'm a private investigator, working on behalf of Gianna Tate."

"Right. What can I do for you?"

I cut to the chase. "Was Gianna joining your firm?"

"No." It was a short answer, but I detected the surprise in it, the way his voice rose at the end.

"Why was she visiting your office so frequently if not for—what appears to be—a series of job interviews?"

"That's client-attorney privilege, Ms. Fitzgerald."

My mouth dropped open, and I closed it with a snap. "You're her *attorney*?"

"I'm afraid I can't help you. Now, if there's nothing further?"

"You *do* know she's dead?"

There was a pause, then, "So soon?"

"What do you mean, so soon? She was murdered. On Saturday night."

Another pause, then, "I wasn't aware. But thank you for letting me know."

"So, you're her executor? For her will?"

"Good day, Ms. Fitzgerald." He hung up.

I spent the next hour reverse searching phone numbers Gianna had called frequently over the last six months. Aside from Sante Law in the city, one other number stood out. Athegate Memorial Hospital.

Galloway's face lit up the screen on my phone.

"Hey," I answered, leaning back in my chair. "Good timing."

"Oh?"

"I discovered Gianna has been traveling to the city frequently, monthly basically, over the last six months."

"Any idea why?"

"Well, at first, I thought maybe she was going to retire. Cos, you know, she'd pretty much stopped taking on new clients. Going through her planner, I found she'd blocked out time in the city every month, so I figured she was going to move there, figured she was looking at properties, that sort of thing."

"So, that's where that ended up."

Oops. I forgot I'd swiped the planner from Galloway. "You can have it back. I'm done with it."

"Oh, I intend to. But you've screwed up the chain of custody."

Oops again. "Anyway," I continued, "I discovered she's been visiting another law firm—Sante Law—so I called to find out if she intended to work there. It turns out she's their *client*."

"I guess attorneys need their own lawyers from time to time."

"Do they? Anyway, she'd been meeting with Bradley Howard, but he wouldn't tell me why—client confidentiality and all that."

Galloway snorted. "Can't imagine that stopping you. Have you asked her about it? Is she there?"

"Nah, she swung by for a bit, but she's gone again. She's the most unusual ghost I've ever worked with. She can open doors!"

"Imagine," he drawled, clearly not as impressed as I was.

"Anyway, she was also calling the Athegate Memorial Hospital regularly, so I'm thinking maybe she has a sick friend or relative in the city and is helping get their affairs in order, hence taking all this time off and traveling to the city, etc."

"You would think she'd take care of the will and estate planning herself," Galloway pointed out. "After all, that is what she does."

"Conflict of interest?" It was flimsy. Of course, if you had a terminally ill friend, you'd help get their legal affairs in order. "Anyway, you called me. You got news?"

"I figured you'd be interested that we got the results back from what we thought was grease on the island bench in Gianna's dressing room."

"And?"

"Not grease. Makeup."

"Makeup?" I frowned. "Like... eyeliner? Mascara?" I'd never seen either of those things leave a smear like that before.

"Stage makeup. Like face paint," he clarified.

"Oh." I nodded. Then the penny dropped. "Oh!"

"Exactly. Gianna wasn't wearing stage makeup, so it couldn't have been hers. It had to be one of the guests at the party."

I ran through my mind, trying to remember who was wearing stage makeup. Amanda and Dustin with their vampire costumes, Carolyn and Chloe with their Day of the Dead costumes, and the two zombies, Jack and Caitlin. Our suspect pool had narrowed considerably. Only none of them was on my murder board.

The only person from Beasley, Tate, and Associates

I'd flagged with a potential motive had been Chris Haiden, but he hadn't even worn a costume, let alone stage makeup. A quick glance at the clock told me the afternoon had run away from me. If I wanted to question my new list of suspects, I needed to get down to Beasley, Tate, and Associates before everyone left for the day. I tore out of the house so fast that I left a dust trail behind me.

arolyn was in her usual place behind the reception desk when I arrived, and I realized I'd torn down here so fast that I didn't have a concrete plan. Not that that had ever stopped me before, but I was standing in the foyer of a law firm. They weren't going to let me just waltz on in. Which was when I pulled out the one card I didn't want to have to play.

"Is Amanda available?" I asked.

"Do you have an appointment?"

I wasn't aware I needed one. "I'm her sister-in-law."

"Oh, okay." Carolyn smiled. "I'll let her know you're here."

"Thank you." I waited, leaning against the counter while Carolyn dialed Amanda's extension to let her know she had a visitor. "She'll be right out." She smiled at me, the laugh lines at the corners of her eyes deep. Her red lipstick had long since faded, and there was a weariness about her now as if the day had been long, and all she wanted was a glass of wine, a good book, and her cats.

"How are you holding up?" I asked. "With Gianna's passing," I added for clarification.

Her mouth turned down, and she looked despondent. "I can't believe she's gone," she admitted, her eyes welling with tears. "That I'm never going to see her come waltzing through that door again, a whirlwind of activity and just... energy."

"She wasn't so busy lately, though, right? I hear she wasn't taking on many clients."

"I know she had some big project taking up her time, so no, not so many personal clients, but the practice itself is as busy as ever."

The door behind the reception opened, and Amanda stuck her head through. "Oh, hi! Didn't expect to see you. Come on through."

I waved a farewell to Carolyn as I passed and followed Amanda into the inner sanctum. "I didn't get to speak with you when you were here this morning," Amanda said.

"Yeah, I was busy with official police business. Sorry about that."

"Is that why you're here now?"

I frowned. "What? On official police business? Not really." Not the official nor police part anyway.

She indicated a chair in front of her desk, and I sat while Amanda took her seat behind the desk. That's when I noticed it. The bridal magazine, sitting there, taunting me. "What's this?" I pointed to it.

"Oh, I know I'm getting a little ahead of myself, but I couldn't resist a little peek at what's on-trend in wedding gown fashion these days."

Oh boy. Time to nip this in the bud. "You should know that I've hired a wedding planner." There. Rip the Band-aid off. I was expecting shock, horror, anger, and disappointment. I was not expecting the beaming smile.

"That's fantastic. And very smart." She nodded enthusiastically. "What's their name? I'll liaise with them about my ideas."

"Oh. Erm. It's Seb. Sebastian Castle, my neighbor."

She froze for a second, then picked up her phone, typing. "I didn't know he was a wedding planner. I thought he was a teacher."

"He is. But have you seen the man? He has... *style*."

"Are you sure you didn't choose him because his last name is Castle, and you're obsessed with that old TV show?"

"Of course not. That'd be ludicrous." I *had* decided that Seb and I would be BFFs because of it, though.

She paused. "Are we still going dress shopping?"

I chewed my lip. "Let me check in with Seb on that.

He left a flyer on my door—something about a bridal expo in the city?"

Amanda clapped her hands in glee. I looked at her in horror. The Amanda I knew did not act in such a way. She was subdued. Prim. Proper. She talked like she had a plum in her mouth and walked like a stick was stuck up her... you get my drift. She did not clap her hands in delight like a three-year-old at Christmas. She especially didn't clap in delight over anything regarding *mwah*.

Time to change the subject. "Anyway, that's not what I came here for."

"Oh, what's up?"

"It's about Gianna." I lowered my voice and glanced around the open-plan office, not wanting to be overheard.

"What about her?" Amanda matched my tone.

"There was some incriminating evidence left at the crime scene."

"Go on."

"That points the investigation toward one of—"

"One of us?" She was a smart cookie, I'd give her that. "I'm guessing you can't tell me what that evidence is?"

I shook my head.

"How can I help?"

"You're the only one I know who one hundred percent didn't do it." Good thing she couldn't see me crossing my fingers under the desk. "You and Dustin. But I wanted to ask about some of your colleagues. Possible motives, that type of thing."

"Oh. Sure. Perhaps we'll duck into a meeting room, hmm?"

"Great idea."

She picked up a yellow legal pad and led the way into a private meeting room with a round table and four chairs. After we were both seated, she looked at me, waiting.

"Let's start with Carolyn."

Amanda nodded. "Of course. It's logical she's a suspect. She found the body." She tapped her pencil on the legal pad, thinking. "As for motive, not coming up with much, I'm afraid. Carolyn is happy in her job, as far as I'm aware. She does a darn good job of it too, let me tell you."

"So, no ill feelings when Chloe came on board?"

Amanda rolled her eyes. "Oh, there was some tension, to begin with, sure."

"Tension? I thought Carolyn wasn't interested in the Office Manager position?"

Amanda stopped tapping the pencil, her head tilting to the side. "What makes you say that?"

"I checked the personnel files. Carolyn didn't apply for it."

The pencil tapping started up again. "Yeah, there was an unfortunate misunderstanding about that." She dropped the pencil and leaned back in her chair. "Apparently, Carolyn spoke with Gianna privately about the newly created vacancy. Gianna told her she didn't need to officially put in an application, that she'd consider her anyway."

"So, she *did* want the job?"

Amanda shrugged. "I think maybe she did. When Chloe was appointed, Carolyn had it out with Gianna, who said she didn't recall any such conversation with her, so she wasn't even considered."

"Ouch."

"Yeah. Then, I think just to save face, Carolyn pretended she didn't really want the role and was perfectly happy staying receptionist."

It tied in with what Gianna had already told me. Carolyn must've misunderstood, for Gianna certainly hadn't thought the older woman was looking for a promotion. But a heck of a misunderstanding from Carolyn's perspective.

"Plus, that was months ago," Amanda pointed out. "Hardly a motive to act on any disgruntled feelings now."

My thoughts exactly. "And what about Chloe? Any grievances with Gianna?"

"Not a one that I'm aware of. She settled in quickly. She's a fast learner, friendly, and personable. She passed her probation with no issues. And she works really well with Carolyn. They get on together and make a great team when it comes to the administration side of things."

"That brings me to Jack Ayers. And his wife, Caitlin."

"The dynamic duo." She cupped her chin, deep in thought. "I'm not aware of any problems with Gianna or anyone else in the firm. Obviously, they work well together—not all married couples do. But they live for their boys, Christian and Alexander."

"So, no motive that you can think of?"

"No. Sorry."

"And everyone was in the ballroom the entire time?"

Amanda sighed. "I wish I could say one hundred percent that no one snuck out, but the truth is, I guess they could have. It's not like I was being hyper-vigilant. Someone may have ducked out to use the bathroom or something and only been gone for a minute or two. But I didn't notice anyone missing."

My sigh was heartfelt. "Okay, thanks."

Do you know what I hate? Dead ends. They're even worse than split ends. And I'd just hit a dead end.

Amanda glanced at her watch, then gathered her legal pad and pencil and stood. "Sorry, but it's getting late, and I need to pick up the kids from daycare. We can continue this later at home if you like?"

I stood, pushing in my chair. "I might just have to take you up on that. I'll let you know, okay?"

"Sure." She ushered me out of the meeting room with a hand on my shoulder. In my ear, she whispered, "If anyone asks, we were wedding planning."

I bit back the groan that rose up my throat and threatened to spill out. I had a feeling Amanda was going to be a bridezilla-by-proxy, and I was at a total loss on how to deal with her. I'd thought hiring Seb as my wedding planner would firmly establish boundaries, but instead, she'd embraced it wholeheartedly. I thought I may just owe Seb an apology for the potential harassment coming his way.

***

Galloway beat me home. Not only that, he was cooking! Have I mentioned how much I love this man?

"What's this?" I asked, coming up behind him and sliding my arms around his waist. I peered around him to try and get a peek into the skillet.

"Hey." He paused to give me a kiss. "I know between the Gianna stuff and the wedding stuff that you probably haven't been eating very well lately, so I figured I'd cook something delicious and healthy."

I glanced toward the pantry, which thankfully had remained closed. Had he found my Cheez-It stash? Everyone else had. I didn't see the problem. Cheese was healthy. Kinda.

"Thanks, babe." I tried to inject the correct amount

of enthusiasm and appreciation into my voice. It wasn't that I was ungrateful. It was that I didn't need yet another person on my back about eating healthier. I was fine. My high caffeine intake was fine. My junk food obsession was fine.

Galloway burst out laughing. "I'm teasing, you goose. As if I'd force you to eat healthy food."

I punched him in the arm. "Not fair. So, what are you making?"

He stepped aside to reveal the burgers and bacon sizzling in the pan. "Mmmm." I breathed in deep. "Delish."

"Go get washed up. These are almost done."

"Yes, Mom." He swatted me on the rear for my insolence, but I dutifully headed to the bathroom to wash and dry my hands. "Where are Bandit and Thor?" I called.

"Out back. I brought them a treat."

I finished in the bathroom and retreated to the back deck, watching Thor and Bandit on the lawn.

"Whatcha got?" I asked them.

"I've got pecans!" Bandit declared, holding one between her paws to show me.

"Yum." I grinned, enjoying her enjoyment. "What about you, Thor?"

Thor was rolling around on the grass in apparent ecstasy.

"I'm proper soused," he drawled, his British accent

thick.

"Proper soused? What does that even mean?"

"I think he's drunk," Bandit said. "He's talking funny, and he's acting weird."

Not drunk. High. "Do you have catnip?" I asked the inebriated cat.

"Oooooh yeeeaaahhhh." He rolled around some more, apparently in seventh heaven.

Returning inside, I accepted the glass of wine Galloway had left on the counter.

"You're home early." Sliding onto the stool at the breakfast bar, I drank my wine, watched my man cook, and thought about how perfect my life was. "I thought you'd be tied up with this latest piece of evidence."

Glancing at me over his shoulder, he poked at the food with a spatula in one hand and cradled his glass of wine in the other. "Do I assume that's what you were doing? Where were you anyway? Beasley, Tate, and Associates?"

"Good guess."

"And?"

I heaved out a breath. "Nothing. From my new suspect pool, none of them have a motive. I guess they all had the opportunity, yet no one can say for sure if anyone left the ballroom. You?"

"So, forensics came back on the swab and identified it as stage makeup. We're waiting on further tests to see if they can identify what sort, even try and narrow it down to a brand."

"They can do that?"

"They can try, but it may take a while."

"Then what? You compare everyone's makeup to the sample?"

"If that's what it takes."

I began ticking off on my fingers. "We know Gianna was having regular meetings with Bradley Howard from Sante Law. She was also calling the Athegate Memorial Hospital on the regular—"

"Was she visiting there too?" Galloway cut in. "Not just calling?"

"It would make sense if she was," I said. "It's in the city, so maybe that's why she was doing business with Sante Law… because she was visiting her sick friend or relative in the hospital, so why not use a local attorney for their needs?"

"I'm still puzzled why she wouldn't take care of business herself." Galloway put down his wine and slid the burger patties onto the buns he had ready and waiting. "The only thing I can think of is that she needed a lawyer, personally."

I looked at him, my mind whirling. "Maybe Gianna is the sick one," I whispered. "But she didn't want anyone to know." I put down my glass of wine without knocking it over—a miracle—and pushed back my chair. "I need Ben."

"He's not here?" Galloway finished putting together the burgers and slid one of the plates in front of me.

"I am now." Ben appeared next to him, resting his hand on Galloway's shoulder.

"Don't you feel that?" I asked Galloway, my eyes going from his shoulder to his face and back again.

"Feel what?" Picking up his burger, he took a huge bite.

"Ben has his hand on your shoulder. Whenever he touches me, I get this icy cold sensation. Impossible to miss."

"Nah, sorry," he said through a mouthful of food. "Sorry, Ben."

"No worries, man." Ben patted him on the back and then moved to stand opposite us. "What's up?"

"Can you check the patient records at Athegate Memorial Hospital to see if Gianna was a patient?"

"Sure. Your computer on?"

"Yep."

Ben got to work while Galloway and I stuffed our faces with the best burgers I'd ever had. It was handy having his supernatural abilities, that's for sure. He got into records I'd never get access to without anyone knowing. Which gave me another idea.

"Hey!" I yelled, making Galloway jump and clutch a hand to his ear.

"Sorry," I whispered. "Ben is in the office, and I just thought of something else I need his help with."

"A little warning next time." Galloway shuddered and thumped the side of his head. As if my voice was that loud! Pft.

"Ben," I called in a moderately quieter voice. "Can you also get into Harry Watts's financials? I want to know where he got the money for the lease on his new gym."

"Sure," Ben called back.

"You're still digging into Harry? He has a solid alibi. He's not our killer."

"No, I know. I just want to know for my own sake because it doesn't make sense. It's a mystery that needs to be solved. The bank didn't lend him that money, so where did it come from? Is he dealing drugs? Selling counterfeit art?"

"Maybe someone else loaned him the money."

"Like a loan shark?" Dangerous territory for Harry Watts if that were the case. Miss a payment, and you were likely to find yourself with a broken kneecap or two.

"You always go to worst-case scenario." Galloway nudged me with his elbow, much like Ben does, only his touch was warm and solid, and I nearly slid off the stool. "Maybe Harry Watts had an unexpected inheritance and came by the money legitimately?"

"You're kidding, right?" I snorted, righting myself. "Anyway, that can't be the case. Why was he arguing with Gianna at lunch on Saturday about the loan when he'd already signed the lease and was moving stuff in?"

Galloway finished his burger, cheeks bulging. "Fair point," he mumbled through the mouthful. At least that's what I think he said.

"You guys might want to come and see this!" Ben hollered.

Putting down my half-eaten burger, I stood. "Come on," I said to Galloway. "Ben's found something."

He'd found something all right. On the monitor was a patient record from the Athegate Memorial Hospital. Galloway and I leaned in to read it.

"It's Gianna's," he said.

"Yeah... oh man."

"Astrocytoma," Ben confirmed. "Which is a grade IV glioblastoma multiforme."

"Which is?" I asked.

"Brain tumor," Ben and Galloway both answered.

"Diagnosed six months ago." Galloway kept reading. "No treatment. It was offered, and she refused. She was terminal."

"Why turn down treatment?" I wondered.

"Possibly because the treatment is unpleasant, not to mention side effects. Possibly worse than the illness. And if you're terminal, you have to weigh quality of life over quantity."

"Does it say how long they thought she had?" I asked.

"A year at the most," Ben said.

"A year. Can you imagine? How do you cope with being told you'll be dead within a year? The poor woman."

"Death comes for all of us," Ben said somberly. "Whether you see it coming or not."

"Sorry, Ben, I didn't mean—" I began, but he cut me off.

"It's all good, Fitz. I know you didn't mean anything by it. But you're right. Cancer sucks, no matter which way you look at it."

"So, she wasn't helping a friend tie up her affairs. She was preparing for her own demise," Galloway said. "Hence the lawyer."

"Of course."

"If you're done reading this, I'll check Harry Watts's financials as requested." Ben pointed to the screen, and I waved at him to proceed.

"Sure, go ahead." Turning to Galloway, I said, "You don't think Gianna took her own life, do you?"

"You mean died on her own terms rather than waiting for the tumor to ravish her body? Sadly, in this case, no. The angle of the stab wound means it would be impossible to inflict on yourself. That and the murder weapon would have been left behind. No, this wasn't a suicide. Someone stabbed her and took whatever they used to do the deed with them."

"What if she enlisted someone to kill her? Suicide by someone else."

"Still makes it murder. And honestly, if you convinced a friend to assist in killing you, you wouldn't have them stab you. You'd take an overdose and drift off to sleep."

"Assisted dying." Ben nodded. "I've heard of it. And Galloway's right. You wouldn't choose stabbing. It hurts."

"And Gianna wasn't at that point. She was still functional. If she wanted to die, she was capable of doing it herself."

"Both fair points." So, we agreed that Gianna was murdered. We were still no closer to finding out by whom, despite learning that she was terminally ill. It seemed incredibly unfair that her last few good months were snatched from her. It also explained her erratic ghostly behavior. The tumor was manifesting in unusual ways in the afterlife.

"I wonder if she even remembers that she was ill," I said to no one in particular. "Surely, she would have mentioned it to me otherwise."

"I can't even begin to imagine what it's like for you, dealing with ghosts daily," Galloway said, wrapping his fingers around the nape of my neck and massaging away the tension he found there. "And from what you've told me, Gianna seems to be a bit of a handful, which might be the tumor at play. Or maybe it's just her demeanor."

"Impossible to say until we ask her," Ben said. "Here. Look. Harry Watts's bank account."

I drew Galloway's attention to the screen. "Look. Wow. One hundred thousand dollars was deposited into Watts's account last week. It says international deposit. Can you trace that?"

"Give me a few minutes. I'll see if I can follow the path." The screen flickered and shimmered as Ben did his thing, following the bank transaction's meta trail.

"I'm not even sure this can be classified as illegal," Galloway said while watching the static monitor. "You're not actually doing anything. It's all Ben. And he's non-living, so technically... we're in a gray area for sure."

"Why? You thinking of ratting me out to the cops?" I teased.

"No, I'm trying to think up reasonable explanations to cover my own butt should any of this ever be needed in a court of law."

"You think the money is dirty?"

"International deposit? It doesn't sound good. I'm thinking drug money, laundered through an offshore bank account."

"Well then, you'd be wrong," Ben chimed in. "This money was bounced through an offshore account, but it originated from a Sante Law trust account."

I gasped. "What?"

"What is it?" Galloway asked.

"That money!" I pointed to the screen. "It came from a trust account from Sante Law. Where Gianna's attorney, Bradley Howard, works." I turned to Ben. "Do you think you can go find Gianna, bring her back here? This'll be easier if I could just ask her directly."

He shrugged. "Sure." And he disappeared.

18

"*H*ere she is." Ben returned half an hour later, Gianna in tow. This time, she was dressed in a teal-colored playsuit with a matching longline cardigan that swished around her ankles as she walked. Stunning and stylish as always.

"You wanted to see me?" she asked. We'd retreated to the living room, enjoying another glass of wine while pondering who had killed Gianna. We still didn't have a firm suspect, and that rankled. We were managing to put together a picture of Gianna's life but not her killer.

"Gianna," I said, louder than necessary to draw Galloway's attention to the fact that we had her ghost in our presence. "We hear you were ill. An astro..." I trailed off, trying to recall the name of her cancer.

"Astrocytoma," Galloway chimed in.

"Yes, that's it. An astrocytoma. Do you remember that?"

She sat in the armchair she'd occupied earlier and crossed her legs, looking at me. "You know, now that you mention it, yes, I think there was something."

"Were you seeing a doctor at Athegate Memorial Hospital?"

Her face lit up. "Why yes. Yes, I was. Oh, he was a lovely fellow. Now, what was his name? Doctor Thomas Murray."

"And were you receiving treatment?"

She shook her head. "No. I went in every month for a scan and to track my progress and discuss palliative care options, end of life plan, that sort of thing."

"Why no treatment?"

She snorted. "I have an incurable brain tumor. Why put myself through treatment? Surgery wasn't an option. It was inoperable, with tentacles of the beastly thing snaking through my brain. They'd do more damage than good. Chemo? That stuff is toxic and would make me feel like death, and it wouldn't cure me, only postpone the inevitable. Same with radiation. Burn my skin, lose my hair, for what? A miserable few extra weeks or months? No, thank you."

"What's she saying?" Galloway whispered in my ear.

"I'll tell you later," I whispered back. To Gianna, I said, "Tell us about your attorney. Bradley Howard. You saw him each time you went to the city for your medical appointments, didn't you?"

"Yes, he's another good man. I was setting up my living will, what would happen with my estate upon my death. You know. The usual."

"Is that why you gave a hundred thousand dollars to Harry? And why you didn't sign the loan because he obviously no longer needed it? Was that what you were even fighting about?"

She smiled. "My faith in you was not misplaced. You've found all my secrets."

I snorted. "Hardly. But please," I waved a hand, "continue."

"Yes, I gifted the money to Harry. Why wait until I was dead when he could use it now? And yes, we argued. Only because Harry wasn't happy with the strings attached to it. All told, his inheritance from me is five hundred thousand dollars. One hundred thousand in advance. The rest will be released to him on a yearly basis after my death."

"Why not give him the whole shebang now?"

She laughed. "Because the man has no business sense, and he'd blow it on stupid things. I knew he needed an injection of serious capital if he was going to succeed in getting this venture off the ground. The money comes with strings, as I said. He is to use the services of a business advisor—vetted by Bradley."

"Ahh, now it makes sense." I turned to Galloway and repeated what she'd told me.

"Smart." Galloway nodded in approval.

"That's why you weren't taking on new clients, wasn't it? Because you were unwell. Why did you agree to represent June?"

"Agreeing to represent June was one of the reasons I realized the tumor was affecting my judgment. I'd be doing my clients a disservice if I continued to accept them. You see, it was her dog. Her dog swayed me, and that's not how I choose my clients. It was an early warning sign."

"One that you were smart enough to recognize."

She inclined her head. "I didn't want word getting out. I'd tell people when I was ready. So, I had Jack do most of the leg work, with Caitlin preparing the court documents. And if I wasn't well enough to attend court, or if I felt I'd be putting June at risk, Jack would step in."

"But he didn't know you were sick?"

"No. Everyone thinks I have this big project happening in the city taking up all my time and attention."

"The big project being your brain tumor, I take it."

"Exactly." A glass of wine materialized in her hand, and she took a sip. "Then there was that stupid blackmail attempt."

"Oh! I can't believe I haven't told you! We caught him."

"You did?"

"Yes. It was, of all people, Adam Harris. Your reputation as a cut-throat attorney was too much for him. He knew he would lose the case, but he thought if he could distract you with the blackmail thing, you'd either hand the case off to someone else or just lose because you weren't on your game."

She tipped back her head and laughed, long and loud. "Oh, if only he knew."

"Right?" I grinned. "But if it's any consolation, I think he regretted it as soon as he'd done it, and he had no intentions of following through. He didn't have any nude photos of you."

"I'd offer to write you a check for services rendered, but you know...." She waved a hand, indicating her incorporeal self, and laughed again.

"All we need to do now is find your killer."

It was sobering. We'd unwound so much of Gianna's puzzle, but this last piece? It was missing, and until it was found, she wouldn't be able to cross over and find peace.

"Gianna?" Galloway suddenly piped up, making me jump as I hadn't expected him to join in the conversation. "Do you remember what happened to your phone? At the party on Saturday night, at your house, did you have it on you? Perhaps took it upstairs with you when your necklace broke?"

"Honey," she drawled, "I *always* have my phone with me. It's on my nightstand when I sleep and either in my hand or in my purse when I'm awake."

"She says yes," I whispered from the corner of my mouth. "She always has it with her."

"Ben?" Galloway asked, and I obligingly pointed to where Ben was standing. Galloway turned in his direction. "Can you find Gianna's phone? We've had no luck, so it must be off, or the battery is dead, meaning we can't trace the signal. Can you?"

Ben shook his head. "Nah, man. I need a device to be operational. If it's turned off, it may as well be a brick."

"He says no. Like you guys, he needs it to be on to access it."

"Okay, Gianna, I need you to think." Galloway turned his attention to the armchair. "What was the last thing you did with your phone?"

She tapped a manicured finger against her lips. "Let me see. I remember my necklace breaking and being annoyed. I went upstairs to put it away for safekeeping. I pulled out another necklace and held it against my chest to see if it went with my dress."

This was new. She hadn't mentioned this before. I kept my lips clamped shut unless I disrupted her train of thought, and she lost the memory.

"I remember taking a selfie," she said. "My eyes— you see, sometimes I can't see so well. Part of the tumor presses on my optic nerve, and I couldn't tell if the necklace looked okay or not when I looked in the mirror. But with a selfie, I can enlarge the image."

I was impressed. "Smart," I encouraged.

"Thank you." She beamed, pleased with the praise. "So, yes, I was facing the mirror, my back was to the door, but I couldn't see my reflection very well, so I took a selfie. That's when Carolyn arrived."

"Carolyn?" I shot upright, backbone rigid.

"Carolyn?" Galloway repeated in my ear.

"Yes," I hissed. "Gianna took a selfie to see if the replacement necklace she'd selected went with her dress, and Carolyn turned up."

"What happened next?" Ben prompted.

Gianna sighed and shook her head. "You know, Carolyn really wasn't herself. She was angry."

"Angry? What about?"

"That's what I don't understand. She was ranting about me hiring someone else, that she was missing out on the chance of another promotion, and how dare I do that to her again and didn't I value her as a friend and an employee."

"Were you? Hiring someone else?"

"No, of course not! Why would I? If anything, Felix may want to hire another lawyer to cover my absence, but that was his call, not mine. Anyway, Felix didn't know I was ill, nor did he know that I left my share of the business to him, so there was no way Carolyn could know."

"So, she *was* mad when you hired Chloe?"

Gianna nodded. "That's when I initially started to think something was wrong. Because Carolyn swore up, down, and sideways that we'd had a conversation about her becoming office manager and we'd hire a new receptionist, and apparently, I was on board with it, but I have zero recollection of that conversation."

"And you don't think Carolyn was lying?"

She shook her head. "Absolutely not. Carolyn has been with us from the very first day we opened the doors. No, I'm sorry to say, my memory lapse was on me. That's the first time I thought something might be up, but I didn't think brain tumor. I thought maybe dementia or something? A few other symptoms eventually turned up. Headaches. Sense of smell and taste. Foods I loved suddenly smelled vile. So, I saw a doctor in the city. I didn't want anyone in Firefly Bay knowing I was losing my marbles."

"So, not remembering that you'd agreed to give Carolyn the office manager job, you advertised the vacancy, conducted interviews, and eventually appointed Chloe. You didn't ask Carolyn why she hadn't applied?"

She shrugged. "Nope. I figured if she wanted the job, she'd have put in an application or at least spoken to me about it. Trust me, I felt awful about it. I gave her an extra bonus at Christmas to make up for it."

"But you never told her why? Why you couldn't remember?"

"No." She heaved a sigh. "Poor judgment on my part, but in my own defense, my mind wasn't my own."

"Do you remember her stabbing you?"

Gianna looked me dead in the eye. "I do not. And you know what? I'm glad. I'm thankful that that isn't the last memory I have of her. We were friends. I feel terrible that I drove her to it."

I twisted to look at Galloway. "We need to go and speak with Carolyn."

"I'm guessing I'm going to need a search warrant."

"Correct. Unless she confesses, of course."

"I'm coming too!" Gianna declared, standing up and looping her elbow with Ben's as they proceeded to head out to my car.

The minute she opened the door and saw Galloway with his badge at the ready, Carolyn Wells knew she was caught. She stepped back, leaving the door open, and said, "You'd better come in."

"Isn't her house lovely?" Gianna swept inside, walking right through me, which had my heart freezing in my chest. I wheezed, doubling over while I waited for the shock of it to pass.

"Okay?" Galloway whispered, grabbing hold of my elbow in case I toppled forward onto the floor.

"Urgh," I assured him.

"I'm going to look around," Ben said, shuffling past me so I didn't receive a second dose.

"I just love the quaint seaside country vibe she's created," Gianna gushed, darting from one object to another. "Small, though."

Carolyn's cottage was indeed both lovely and small. Tastefully decorated with a beach theme, as Gianna had pointed out. Two cats lay sleeping on the back of the sofa, and I recalled someone telling me Carolyn enjoyed reading and cats.

"I suppose you're here to arrest me?" Carolyn asked, holding out both wrists, waiting to be cuffed. I glanced at Galloway, wondering if he'd oblige and slap the cuffs on her. He didn't. He pointed to a chair and demanded she sit.

"Walk me through what happened."

"I didn't mean to kill her," she whispered, drawing in a shuddering breath, tears filling her eyes and overflowing, running down her cheeks, leaving mascara streaks in their wake. That's when it hit me. The black smudge of makeup in Gianna's dressing room. I had seen that black smudge before on the back of Carolyn's hands. The painted on Day of the Dead skeleton. I'd noticed it was smudged when everyone was gathered in the ballroom, but I'd put it down to her wringing her hands. The proof had been there all along, only I hadn't realized what it meant.

"But I was so mad, and she didn't even care!"

"About what?" I asked.

"She was hiring someone else! It wasn't an attorney, or I would've known about it, but no, I'd seen it for myself, so when she said she wasn't hiring anyone, I knew she was lying, and I just... I just saw red."

"When was this? When did you find out she was hiring someone else?"

"Friday. In her office. She said she had some mail that needed to go out, and Jessica was on her lunch break—she normally brings Gianna's mail out to reception—so I figured I'd duck in and grab it. Her planner was open on the desk, I didn't mean to snoop, but I saw it there, and I couldn't unsee it."

Oh, my giddy aunt! I knew what she'd seen.

"Hire Audrey. Right there, in the planner. Check for yourself."

Galloway shot me a look and used a cutting motion across his throat, meaning, keep my mouth shut, don't say a word. I clamped my lips as tightly closed as possible, so tight they practically disappeared.

"What happened next?"

"I confronted her about it, and she denied all knowledge. She was lying to me. Again! I couldn't believe it." She cried louder now, the tears no longer silent but long, loud sobs that spoke of her hurt.

"Oh, honey," Gianna tried to comfort her, but Carolyn had no idea the other woman was there.

"I told myself to sleep on it. To calm down. Approach her again when I was in a clearer state of mind."

"So, you followed her up to her bedroom the night of the party."

"No. I talked to her in the ballroom. But again, she had no idea what I was talking about. She said she wasn't hiring anyone and that we had enough staff. But I *saw* it. In her planner. *Hire Audrey*. She claimed she didn't know anyone called Audrey."

"Oh, dear," Gianna whispered, her hand covering her mouth. She shot a distraught look my way. "I shouldn't have let it come to this. I should have told them."

I gave a half shrug, unable to answer her.

"I was... I was *shaking* with rage. So, when her necklace broke, and she went upstairs to change it, I snatched the ice pick from the bar and followed."

I was frozen in my seat, half fascinated, half horrified. Gianna plopped down next to me, apparently feeling the same if the expression on her face was anything to go by. She turned to me. "You know, I really thought it was just a random low life who'd killed me for some perceived injustice. Possibly the stupid blackmailer. I never thought it was anyone from my family. Oh, poor Carolyn, she must have been so hurt by my behavior, thinking I'd do that to her, betray her, again. I should have told her the truth. This is all on me."

I had to practically chew my lips off to keep from answering her. Yes, the whole situation was sad, but Carolyn didn't have to stab her. That was all on Carolyn, but I couldn't tell Gianna that. Not yet.

"Then what happened?" I realized Galloway needed her to say it. He needed her whole confession.

"She was taking selfies," Carolyn snorted. "Of all things. And then she saw me and turned around and asked me what I wanted, and I said I want you to tell me the truth about Audrey, and she said, 'Who's Audrey?' And I..." She drew in a shuddering breath. "I stepped forward and rammed the ice pick into her belly."

The shuddering breath was released on a groan. "She, she, she just looked at me with this shocked expression, and then she pulled the ice pick out...and handed it to me. I took it from her. I didn't know what else to do, so I took it from her because she handed it to me. She didn't say a word. Then she collapsed, and her phone fell from her hand, so I grabbed it, shoved the phone and the ice pick in my pocket, wiped any blood off my hands—easy to do when you're wearing a black dress. Then I screamed for help."

"And no one else noticed that you'd followed her out of the ballroom?" Galloway asked.

"Everyone was in shock. It was easy to plant the seed that I hadn't gone upstairs until the car had arrived to take us to the Scarecrow Ball. I think I noticed the flash of the headlights sweeping across the foyer as I was going upstairs. So, I used it. I told the others I'd seen the car arrive and had gone upstairs to get Gianna."

"Why take her phone?"

"Because I'm pretty sure I'm in one of the selfies she took."

"Spot on." The words slipped out, and I mimed locking my lips and throwing away the key when Galloway shot me a look. But Carolyn was right, for Gianna remembered precisely that.

"Only," Carolyn barked out a laugh, "I couldn't unlock the damn thing to delete the photo because she has it set to facial recognition."

"That's in case I couldn't remember my pin code," Gianna told me.

"Before I arrest you," Galloway said solemnly, "there's something you should know."

"Oh?" She plucked a tissue from the box next to her chair and blew her nose. "What's that?"

"This," he pointed to me, "is Audrey."

Carolyn's brow furrowed. "What? What do you mean? Aren't you a police officer?"

"I'm a private investigator. And Gianna hired me to find out who was attempting to blackmail her."

"What?" Carolyn screeched. "You can't be."

"I'm sorry." And I was. What a horrible set of misunderstood circumstances all the way around. "And there's something that Gianna probably should have told you. I know she intended to, but she left it too long, and now she can't. But what you don't know, none of you know, is that Gianna was ill. Terminally ill. She had an incurable brain tumor. Some things, like her not remembering her conversation with you about the office manager job? Those were symptoms of her condition."

"Oh my God, that's terrible!" Carolyn promptly burst into tears, great big gulping sobs of emotion.

"This is terrible," Gianna agreed, crossing to her friend and rubbing her back. "It's not her fault, you know. She didn't mean to kill me. If only I'd told her the truth, none of it would have happened."

Galloway let Carolyn cry for a minute before standing and pulling her to her feet. "Carolyn Wells, you're under arrest for the murder of Gianna Tate." He continued reading her rights while he led her outside. He'd had the foresight to call a patrol car as backup, and it sat at the curb, waiting.

Gianna and I watched through the window as Carolyn was bundled into the back seat. "It doesn't feel like justice was served," Gianna said.

"I know you feel responsible, Gianna, but it all boils down to the fact that she killed you, despite her reasons. She made that decision to stab you with an ice pick. That is one hundred percent on her. She could have chosen a dozen different avenues, but she chose death, and now she has to face the consequences."

"But what about her cats?"

I looked toward the two cats who were still stretched out on the back of the sofa, paying us no heed. "I'll contact Carolyn's family and see if they'll take them."

"Oh, yes, her daughter likes cats. She'll take them for sure. Good. Good."

A bright light filled the room, and I raised my hand to shield my eyes.

"Oh my, look at that. Isn't it gorgeous?"

"Sure is. It's here for you, Gianna. It's time to move on to the next part of your journey."

"Are you coming?" she asked Ben, who'd rejoined us.

He shook his head. "Nah, I'm staying. But you go."

"Okay. Well." She held out her hand, and I attempted to shake it, despite the icy chill her touch evoked. "Thank you for everything. I'm so glad I hired you. Even if it ultimately led to my death." She stepped into the light, leaving me with my mouth hanging open.

"Did she?" I turned to Ben. "Did she just *blame me* for her murder? The cheek!"

Ben laughed. "Come on, you need to tell Galloway the phone and ice pick are still in the pocket of the dress Carolyn wore Saturday night. She hung it up in her wardrobe but failed to get rid of the evidence."

"What's this?" I eyed the overnight bag sitting by my front door. It had been three days since we'd wrapped up Gianna's case, and Galloway had been kept busy 'crossing the t's and dotting the i's' the entire time.

"We're having a little getaway." Galloway beamed. "You don't have to worry about a thing."

I immediately worried. "But I haven't packed."

He pointed to the overnight bag. "I packed for you."

My brow furrowed. The scabs from my scratches having fallen off the day before meant I could do so with no discomfort. I wasn't sure whether I liked that he'd packed for me or if it was the most thoughtful gift he could ever give me. But I was warming up to the idea of a getaway. "So, where are we going?"

"Chicago."

"Oh." I knew my voice revealed my disappointment. I was thinking tropical beach or a mountainside cabin. Not Chicago. I wasn't much of a city girl. "Okay."

Galloway belted out a laugh, pulled me into a bear hug, and then said the words I'd been dreading. "I'm taking you to meet my family. Now that Mom and Dad are back from Australia, Mom wants to meet you. Before the wedding."

We'd been in our own little bubble in Firefly Bay, albeit my family was in the bubble with us. Of course, it was only fair that I met Galloways' family. It had never come up before, and I'd treated the whole situation as if Galloway were an orphan with no family of his own—which was wrong of me. But he rarely talked about his folks that it slipped my mind that they existed. Not to mention his Mom and Dad had been living on the other side of the world when we first met.

"Plus, it's Mom's birthday. I figure she'd appreciate a visit from her prodigal son."

"It's her birthday!" I slugged him in the arm, hard. "Why is this the first I'm hearing of this? Man, you're making me look like a bad daughter-in-law. I haven't gotten her a gift, let alone a card."

"Meeting you is gift enough."

"Shut up." I shoved him, mad. I wanted to make a good impression when I eventually met his folks, and this wasn't it. "Is she having a party? Will it be a big affair?"

"Relax." He tried to wrestle me back into a hug, but I resisted, ducking and weaving. "It's going to be fine. And no big party, it will just be us."

"Just us?"

"Is that a bad thing?"

"It means we're going to be under a microscope. All the attention will be on us."

"Babe, we're getting married. Of course, all the attention will be on us. It's going to be fine, I promise. This is why I kept it as a surprise, so you couldn't work yourself up into knots beforehand."

"What if they don't like me?"

This time when he attempted to pull me in for a hug, I let him. My fear was real. What if his family didn't like me? What if they felt I wasn't good enough for their son?

"They are going to love you! How could they not? Babe, I wish you could see yourself the way I see you. Brave, fearless, beautiful. You are a goddess."

"I'm a clumsy slob," I protested.

"That too," he conceded with a laugh and a kiss to show he was teasing. "But that's what makes you uniquely you. I wouldn't want you any other way and trust me, my family will love you as much as I do. Maybe even more so." He sobered.

Looping my arms around his neck, I gave in. "Well, Galloway, you asked for it. Tell your folks to brace themselves. Audrey Fitzgerald is coming to Chicago."

THE END

AFTERWORD

Thank you for reading, if you enjoyed **Wild Ghost Chase**, please consider leaving a review. You can find a complete list of my books, including series and reading order on my website at:

www.JaneHinchey.com

Also, if you'd like to sign up to receive emails with the latest news, exclusive offers, and more, you can do that here:

www.JaneHinchey.com/subscribe

And finally, I'd love to invite you to join my **VIP Readers group** where you get exclusive access to me, the opportunity to win one of the monthly signed paperback giveaways, join in live videos, get sneak peeks at works in progress and so much more.

www.JaneHinchey.com/LittleDevils

Thank you so much for taking a chance and reading my book - I do this for you.

xoxo

Jane

READ MORE BY JANE

Find them all at www.JaneHinchey.com/books

The Ghost Detective Mysteries

#1 Ghost Mortem

#2 Give up the Ghost

#3 The Ghost is Clear

#4 A Ghost of a Chance

#5 Here Ghost Nothing

#6 Who Ghost There?

#7 Wild Ghost Chase

Witch Way Paranormal Cozy Mystery Series

#1 Witch Way to Magic & Mayhem

#2 Witch Way to Romance & Ruin

#3 Witch Way Down Under

#4 Witch Way to Beauty & the Beach

#5 Witch Way to Death & Destruction

#6 Witch Way to Secrets & Sorcery

The Midnight Chronicles

#1 One Minute to Midnight

PARANORMAL ROMANCE/URBAN FANTASY

The Awakening Series

ABOUT JANE

Jane Hinchey is an Aussie author who loves to write cozy mysteries with plenty of laughs and mayhem along the way - who says murder can't be fun? Her bestselling Ghost Detective series combines all of this into an intriguing melting pot of paranormal danger, fast-paced action, and plenty of tongue-in-cheek snarky humor.

Jane lives in the mortal realm with her non-paranormal man, two cats whose paranormal status is yet to be determined (she did catch them trying to open a portal in the kitchen that one time), a turtle named Squirt (who is massive!).

Sometimes, when the supernatural chaos calls for a different kind of story, she writes under the name Zahra Stone, where the characters you meet are as sexy as they are deadly.

Learn more or sign up for her newsletter at
www.JaneHinchey.com

CPSIA information can be obtained
at www.ICGtesting.com
Printed in the USA
BVHW030814150223
658553BV00016B/101